COMPULSION

JENNIFER CHASE

Outskirts Press, Inc.
Denver, Colorado

Outskirts Press, Inc.
http://www.outskirtspress.com

ISBN: 978-1-4327-3416-9

Library of Congress Control Number: 2008938445

Outskirts Press and the "OP" logo are trademarks belonging to Outskirts Press, Inc.

PRINTED IN THE UNITED STATES OF AMERICA

To my husband Mark for his patience,
understanding, and sense of humor.

Chapter 1
Wednesday 0900 Hours

The man strolls down the gravel driveway to his makeshift torture trap disguised as a late model Chevy Suburban. It is in fact a hideous, retrofitted, rolling snare designed specifically for the secure confinement of the innocent. He has already stalked and captured several children between the ages four and ten from their safe homes and familiar yards. They are never to be seen alive again. Their only mistake was their innocence and inexperience of the inexplicable evil that relentlessly wanders the neighborhoods across the nation, wearing a simple mask of normalcy.

Dressed in khaki shorts, cheap superstore sneakers and a loose fitting blue and yellow Hawaiian shirt, the clean shaven, dark-haired man in his late-thirties looked almost like any other man who might have had a decent day job and perhaps even a family of his own. He doesn't have a single care in the world. He feels a sense of peace and deep relaxation, he's both tired and re-energized.

This particular man has a secret: a dark secret of an unfulfilled need to prey upon the innocent, snatch them from their secure lives, torture them, murder them, and then leave their tiny remains isolated away from civilization. This driving compulsion will never be satisfied, and the hideous crimes will never be fully solved. The police will never find the little victims' remains, and families will never receive closure for their unimaginable loss. Only one promise would prevail, the crimes will continue, remain unsolved and with time eventually be forgotten by the general public. The continuous fantasy re-enactment will never stop as long as the killer is left alive. Death poses the only logical solution to stop this tormenting cycle of death.

He opens the creaky back doors of the Suburban and takes out two white five gallon buckets setting them down on the trash littered street. The back of the vehicle is cluttered with miscellaneous tools and paint supplies that a painting contractor would most likely use. Upon closer inspection, deeper inside the cargo area, there are handcuffs and shackles fixed to stationary hooks reminiscent of medieval torture chambers. The windows are coated with a thin opaque vinyl that ensures complete privacy.

Absently, the man wipes his sweaty forehead with the back of his calloused hand. The temperature has risen past ninety-six degrees, and the heat borders on unbearable; but, typical for Arizona in the beginning stages of the summer months.

The escalating heat works in his favor. The decomposition of the small human bodies will be accelerated in this climate; therefore, omitting the weary task of burying the bodies below a foot deep. The tiny bones left behind will be scattered by scavengers and other small critters leaving no trace of the once lively existence of the innocent victims.

A small red hooded sweatshirt with a decal of Spider Man lays folded on top of one of the white buckets. Covering the top of the other bucket is a pink and purple backpack and a flowered key chain with a single dangling house key never to be used again. The contents inside the buckets is unknown to the naked eye, but secretly stashed underneath is the rest of the children's clothing, shoes, and school supplies. These are the man's valuable trophies drenched with the lingering scent of the victims.

Each of the three little victims was taken from familiar areas between home and school. Their final resting place is only one hundred square miles from the abduction site. Most law enforcement agencies generally are unable to connect together crimes

from larger distances or link one perpetrator, because of understaffing, large workloads, and budget
restrictions. But in reality, most police detectives
aren't trained in serial crimes well enough to be
able to spot the subtle differences in a homicide
crime scene that would indicate a serial homicide or
a one-time homicide.

The man slams shut the doors of the Suburban,
picks up the two buckets and proceeds back up to
the shabby house to stash the belongings in his
basement. In his mind, those items are more cher-
ished than any collected artifact or family heirloom
could ever be to him. He now rests, eats, and then
dreams. The fantasy will slowly begin to replay in
his mind – an endless film of reenactment horrors.
This disease will gain momentum once again and
command more perfect, innocent victims.

Several blocks away, concealed by a couple of
abandoned, rusted out pick up trucks and a partially
torn down grocery store, a high-tech Canon digital
SLR camera with a 500 millimeter telephoto lens
documents every step of the child killer. Extreme
close up photographs are taken of the man, Suburban, tire treads, license plate, dirt residue, bucket
contents, and house with absolute razor-sharp detail.
The complete terrifying story is told without words
and descriptions, but with actions and direct hard
evidence.

An attractive, petite woman with shoulder
length blonde hair stands upright and takes a break
from taking photographs and refocuses her eyes to

the surroundings. She stretches her back and neck. Exhausted from a week and half of stakeouts, she makes her way back to the black Ford Explorer. The heat has taken its toll on her energy and perspiration has soaked through her white t-shirt and stone-washed jeans.

Wishing to be back on the California coast where the air is cool and refreshing, Emily Stone takes three large gulps from a warm bottle of Fiji water. Several empty bottles of water, Gatorade, and diet Coke cans lay on the back seat.

A state-of-the-art Dell notebook computer with several back up hard drives, extra digital cameras, various lenses, video equipment, two store bought cell phones, binoculars, tape recorder, maps, hand scribbled notes, and expanding file with newspaper clippings ride shotgun.

A Glock 9mm Model 17 semiautomatic hand-gun is stashed just within reach with extra clips slipped easily into the map pockets of both front car doors. A Beretta 21 Bobcat Pistol is conveniently concealed in her personal ankle holster, loaded with seven rounds for easy access. Clipped to her belt is a BlackBerry turned to vibrate that alerts her to in-coming text messages, emails and Internet alerts.

Emily knows that her subject will be inside for at least eight to ten hours recharging his strength be-fore finalizing his job and trolling again for new victims. Maybe this time he will lead her to where the tiny gravesites are located. Some serial killers have the need to revisit their victims, especially when they have the overconfidence and arrogance that they will never be caught. Emily relies on this type of criminal behavior to give her the clues and the evidence she needs to stop this pattern of terror. Many serial killers solemnly explain out loud over the improvised graves of their extinguished victims that they are in a better place now, and it was for the better good.

Rubbing her neck and taking a seat behind the wheel, Emily takes a couple of slow even deep breaths from her diaphragm to control her heart rate. She feels an anxious tightening of her neck and body, which in the past has allowed a panic attack to surface during stressful situations. She closes her eyes and counts from one to ten with slow even breaths, and then back from ten to one again. She then opens her eyes, and refocuses her energy on the important task ahead.

Emily turns the engine over and blasts the air-conditioning on her face and torso feeling a sense of reprieve. She had only been to Arizona twice in her thirty-two years of life. With the oven-like stifling heat, she knew why she hadn't returned. Her work had taken her to many states, but her hunt mostly took her to the western states. It was partly due to the higher population aspect, which in turn increases the crime factor and greater possibilities for unsuspecting victims. The FBI estimates that there are forty serial killers roaming the United States at any given time, but Emily knows all too well that number is closer to ten times higher.

This particular case was especially disturbing since the three children had already been murdered and there was nothing that she could do about it. There's a permanent knot in her gut that never loosens, but merely grips her emotions into an unbearable command to keep forging ahead.

Emily has tracked cases throughout Arizona and Nevada about abducted, missing, and mutilated children. It still amazed her how law enforcement agencies who have endless resources at their disposal failed to connect the simple crime patterns just outside their jurisdictions, but well within their investigative reach.

It took Emily less than a day to profile and track down where this particular type of predator would hunt and strike based on the public information of the missing children. Using Internet maps that illustrate parks, malls, and elementary schools, Emily carefully narrowed the search of possible abduction points and easy escape access. She began staking out areas of choice for sex offenders and other types of predators including the names and addresses on the Megan's Law website. With luck and intuition mostly on her side, she was able to find and track the most likely suspect. Sometimes, her hunt took weeks and on one occasion it took two months. This particular hunt took her just under two weeks to track the child murderer, but it was not quite fast enough to save the little victims. This inevitable development in the case only adds to the already heavy burden Emily carries with her every day.

Emily eases the Explorer into drive and leaves the cover of her perfect hiding spot to wait and map out her next move. Her work has only just begun as the child murderer sleeps and dreams of new efficient tortures to use on his next victims. She glances at an open file folder on the passenger seat showing several pictures of missing children. One of the photos shows a smiling freckle-faced boy of seven wearing his favorite red Spider Man sweatshirt.

Chapter 2
Thursday 0530 Hours

Detective Sergeant Ray Rivas diligently priori-
tizes his growing pile of telephone messages
from victims, witnesses, other department detectives, and his demanding Lieutenant. He was also
agonizing over his newest detective, a female officer transplanted from New York City. It's barely
0530 and the Yuma Police Department Homicide
Unit is deserted. Just a soft hum of computers and a
few buzzing fluorescent overhead lights keep him
company until the day shift arrives at 0800 hours.

Detective Rivas has put in more time than all of his other detectives combined in the past six months. Drowning himself in work, it helps him to forget his nasty divorce proceedings and the law firm in charge of his inevitable divorce, or rather his wife's divorce. In his mind, once you're married you stay married no matter what happens. Although being a wife of a cop wasn't always easy, it most certainly wasn't impossible either. There were good times – once.

He tears open the wrapper of an energy bar, takes a bite and then tosses it into the trashcan. The bland piece of cardboard sprinkled with a few peanuts doesn't satisfy his sweet tooth and doesn't taste very healthy either. Instead, he opens his bottom file drawer and retrieves a dark chocolate Milky Way bar. He takes two bites and washes the wonderful silky chocolate down with room temperature police station coffee.

"Now that's a high-energy snack." He muses to himself. He looks at the photo on his desk of two smiling kids at the local water park and his thoughts fall back to the divorce proceedings.

He pushes unpleasant thoughts from his mind and concentrates on his work at hand. He has seen his fair share of homicides over the years and they usually all boiled down to money, jealously or revenge. Two of the worst homicide cases he has seen in his seventeen-year career sat on the right corner of his desk.

The kidnapping, torture, and brutal murder of a

child are what haunt Detective Rivas' dreams, both during the day and at night. To the detective, it keeps the balance of the world in perspective with the steadiness of good versus evil. At least that's what he keeps telling the sarcastic series of thoughts that run in a never-ending loop through his suspicious cop mind.

What's even more disturbing is the epidemic of missing children in the Arizona area over the past year. Every year across the nation there are more than eight hundred thousand children reported missing. That is an unacceptable number in Detective Rivas' mind. Once a runaway or parent abduction is ruled out, there is a whole new breed of predators that begin to emerge in the scenario. The possibilities are endless and disturbingly vile from the kiddie porn industry to sadistic serial murderers that make up more than fifty thousand abducted children each year in the United States. The missing children files for the Yuma area are stacked on the left side of his desk seem to be glaring at him.

The computer terminal behind Detective Rivas softly chimed that there was incoming email, which interrupted his derailed train of cynical thought. He swiveled his chair around to glance at the email subjects on the flat computer screen. There are three listed birthdates of years from 1998 and 2001 with close jurisdictions and cities in several of the subject lines. What's more, the sender consists of four symbol characters that usually represent error messages on most computers.

Detective Rivas squints his eyes and then exhales, "What the hell?"

The firewall and high-tech IT technology for government agencies was supposed to stop any incoming viruses or worms from getting access to their mainframe. Maybe the deviant hackers have found another way to make law enforcement's life a pure hell.

Detective Rivas stares at the computer screen frozen. Snapping out of his trance, he flips open one of the missing person's folder from his desk. He quickly scans the information and shows the date of birth as March 12, 1998 Scottsdale, Arizona. He begins furiously flipping open other folders and matches the missing children's birth dates to the emails on his screen. He blinks his eyes a few times to focus closer on the numbers.

Detective Rivas wastes no more time and clicks on the first email. It quickly loads several photos and a video showing a man clearly digging in a deserted rural area. The detective's blood turns cold and he feels sweat trickle down his neck. He watches the man in the cheap neon Hawaiian shirt talking to himself explaining how sometimes dying is the right thing to do and how brave the little boy was to die for him. A small shadowed body appears in the shallow grave, limp like a rag doll almost too tiny to have been a living and breathing child.

The Detective watches as a photo of the vehicle and license plate, clearly identifiable, comes into view along with other evidence. It was like watching a re-enactment of a cold case file on the Discovery Channel.

Clicking on the other emails, Detective Rivas obtains detailed metro-scan maps from the Yuma county assessors office and clear photographs of the suspect with a complete background of criminal and personal history. An entire detailed investigation unfolds in less than five minutes in front of him from a phantom super sleuth. He notices that all of the emails and their attachments have also been sent to forensic services.

Detective Rivas grabs several of the missing persons files and sprints to the stairwell on his way down to the basement where the forensic identification division is located.

* * * * *

The lights in the corridor are extremely dim due to the fact that there are only a scarce few law enforcement personnel in the building at this early hour. The county government has to pinch more pennies somewhere besides in the hiring and cost of living increases; the next best thing was the utilities.

The dim and deserted hallway eerily echoes with the quick footsteps of Detective Rivas. He is now invigorated with the prospect of catching a child killer or perhaps a serial killer. Many possible scenarios are running through his mind of who actually sent him the information. Was it a retired cop or family member? Maybe it was an angry ex-girlfriend who wanted revenge. It could be the killer himself with a partner who is documenting the crimes for morbid historical purposes.

It is now 0545. Fifteen minutes had barely passed since the first incriminating anonymous emails passed through the police department's computer software firewalls and security encryptions.

Several of the forensic lab doors were closed and dark. Detective Rivas passes the DNA and serology labs. His step quickens as he sees a faint light at the end of the hallway. He knew that it could only mean one thing: the forensic supervisor and criminalist, John O'Brien, worked as many hours at the department as he did. The detective swipes his security card and enters forensic services.

There's a distinct hum that gives the impression that you're in a quiet vacuum and the world is far away. Linear workstations surround much of the perimeter with moveable tables to allow for multiple users of any particular assignment. Each section has been defined for a particular purpose with a gas chromatograph mass spectrometer and a 310 genetic analyzer that allows for examinations of microscopic evidence. A long hallway from one end of the lab to the other gives the layout a cohesive unity and allows for vertical circulation.

Detective Rivas stands illuminated in the doorway and discovers a tall thin man in a white lab coat bent over a scanning electron microscope.

Detective Rivas clears his throat, "John."

The thin man looks up at once and smiles, "Hey detective, I think you have more hours clocked in at this place than I do."

Scarcely able to contain his excitement, "You need to see this." He walks in through the lab and meets the criminalist.

"What's up?" John takes his glasses off, curious because of the detective's intensity. He knew that Detective Rivas was a serious and somewhat conservative police detective.

"Have you checked your email?"

"No, not yet. I try to wait until at least eight before I open that Pandora's box."

"Trust me, you're going to want to pull up your emails right now."

Detective Rivas rolls up a chair next to John, sits down and anxiously waits.

John spins around to his computer workstation and swiftly clicks the mouse twice. Two seconds pass, and his email inbox appears on the screen. He sees the three emails with the unknown sender identification of four strange symbols.

"What the?"

"Trust me, just open the files." Detective Rivas opens his missing children manila files to show John the matching dates of birth.

The computer screen illustrates detailed photographs taken in a crime scene evidence approach of close up, medium, and overall perspectives. John then clicks on the video and once again it reveals an entire chronological crime scene narrative.

John is speechless and barely manages to say, "Wow."

"I need you to verify the authenticity of the images and video while I get the info on the perp and vehicle."

John begins scrolling through the photographs again.

"John can you prioritize this?"

"Yeah, no problem. This is amazing; this is better equipment than we have here in the lab. Not to mention whoever took these is an expert."

"I need to get everything lined up before I go to a judge to get the search and arrest warrant. You good on this?"

"No problem. Give me about two hours."

Detective Rivas smiles, "Not a minute more." He gets to the door.

"Do you have some kind of detective guardian angel watching over you?" John is still impressed looking over the evidence again.

The detective disappears around the corner out of sight to gather all of his information before his detectives begin to arrive.

Chapter 3
Thursday 1900 Hours

The early evening shadows descend on the rural Arizona desert just northeast of Yuma, and the heat of the day is slowly dissipating to a more comfortable level, casting an orange yellow backlit sky. The air is filled with the remnants of well-seasoned soil and native desert plant life from the scorching day.

Just a mile, east at the secondary crime scene of the final resting spot of seven-year-old Randy Jeremiah Johnston, Emily watches the circus-like investigation take shape through binoculars. She is careful not to draw any attention to her vantage spot with any reflection or lights that might catch someone's curious eye. Her heart races and skips an occasional beat. This is the best part of her tedious work watching the events unfold with the reactions of those who are hired to protect and serve.

Police patrol vehicles, crime scene van, four-wheel drive special units, and the coroner scatter around the area of interest. Several uniformed and plainclothes police officers disperse onto the scene in a well-rehearsed manner. Flashlights dance around the vast countryside and large spotlights are being set up by crime scene technicians to search for any possible clues as they secure the area. Several police department civilians carrying silver briefcases filled with portable measuring devices, digital cameras, and other containers for casting and retrieval of evidence get to work. A tall lanky man, obviously a police criminalist, helps to cordon off the specific area of interest and give instructions to less experienced identification technicians.

Without warning, a set of headlights steadily approaches where Emily has carefully hidden herself. She quickly returns to her Explorer, releases the emergency brake and slowly pushes the sport utility vehicle farther into the overgrown brush. Emily tucks herself back against the side of the vehicle and waits for the car to pass.

A police patrol car slowly passes Emily's vantage point, obviously they got lost trying to access the entrance to the crime scene. It's just off rural highway 8 on the dirt bike trails before entering the Anza Trail. Not an easy location to find in the dark. Perhaps they were called to the area to assist with the perimeter security, but more likely they just wanted to view the horrendous crime scene of a serial killer. Emily waits until the police radio is barely audible before she moves from her position.

Emily breathes a sigh of relief and knows her job is done; there is no guesswork or speculation anymore. It is now up to the authorities to determine what happens to this serial killer and how they will proceed. Whether there will be a trial, plea bargain or death penalty, it's out of her hands now. The families can only take slight comfort in knowing what happened to their children. It will never replace their precious child or fill the forever void that is now an inescapable part of their lives.

But it's only a hollow victory for Emily. She is exhausted and wants to get back home as soon as possible. She decides that a break from this entire trauma of events is greatly needed. No more pedophiles, serial killers, missing children, and dead mutilated bodies for a while. Not until the next child abduction. And maybe this time, she'll get there before it's too late. The mere hope is what drives her.

Emily walks back to her Explorer, leans in and turns on the low buzz of activity on the police scanner that sits on the passenger seat. She exits the vehicle again watching the investigation. She puts on lightweight headphones, picks up a listening device and aims the digital sound cannon toward the crime scene and begins recording from her remote computer. After fine-tuning to a particular conversation of significance between two police detectives, Emily listens.

* * * * *

Detective Rivas stands on the edge of the crime scene and takes in everything from left to right and back again. He watches all personnel go about their duties, but he still insists on studying the crime scene personally for his own notes and observations.

Detective William Grant who has only been in Yuma Homicide for six months meets Detective Rivas and waits for instructions. He's a good cop with sound intuitions, but he hasn't had the experience of a massive investigation such as the job they are currently facing.

"I want you to write down everything I say as we walk the crime scene in a grid pattern. Then I want you to observe and speculate what you see after I'm done."

"Is it true that the killer contacted you directly?" The rookie asks.

Detective Rivas stops and looks directly at his rookie detective, "We don't know who sent the information, but for now, let's walk the crime scene."

Detective Grant flips open his notebook, "Ready."

Detective Rivas describes to his rookie partner that the tire tracks lead directly to the gravesite. The vehicle was probably a truck or SUV based on the size and dimension of the tire treads left at the scene. The footprints were completely contaminated; the same set was trampled several times with multiple walks back and forth to the vehicle. This led Detective Rivas to believe, unfortunately, that there would be more than one gravesite and more than one body. He continues his observations and makes brief sketches, while an identification technician takes the proper photographs documenting the entire scene.

John O'Brien instructs one of his best technicians to take a full cup of soil samples from the gravesite and surrounding areas to use as an exemplar to compare to anything found on or with the suspect.

The exhausting task begins for John, he must prepare the crime scene gravesite for excavation of possible evidence. During his entire career, he has had the experience of body excavation in thirty-seven homicides. He expertly sets the datum and grid of the grave areas. The location of any artifacts or evidence from the surface is documented in a notebook and with various photographs.

The tedious task continues as the removal of all surface debris begins in order to locate any possible evidence. John and his assistant begin to sift two inches through twigs, foliage, and soil to get to the first layer of the grave. As he reaches the second layer of the grave, clothing and a small skull appear. This evidence is again documented. It never gets any easier; in fact, it gets more difficult for John. The remains of a small boy are unearthed. For a moment there is strong silence among the crew as they stare into the shallow grave at the tiny broken body.

"John find anything to identify the perp?" Detective Rivas breaks the awkward silence.

"One last possible hiding place", John carefully removes the small body and lays it on a white plastic tarp.

From underneath the body is a perfect footprint impression.

"I'd say a cheap running shoe, size ten."

An identification technician begins to prepare the impression in order to take a complete casting.

A middle-aged petite woman meets up with Detective Rivas, "Detective".

"Dr. Randall, can we get a preliminary educated guess on the manner and cause of death?" Detective Rivas motions to the tiny body.

Dr. Randall is one of the most respected medical examiners from the Yuma County Coroner's office. She has been the expert witness on many cold cases around the globe. Detective Rivas trusts her judgment and respects her opinion.

"There is some inbending where blunt force trauma impacted the frontal part of the skull with some type of tool like a small hammer. There are signs of sexual assault and strangulation, but cause of death was blunt force trauma. Looks like death was between twelve and eighteen hours ago." She looks up at the Detective. "This child was tortured over a period of time and death was not instantaneous."

"There are two more small graves", Detective Rivas replies.

Chapter 4
Friday 0700 Hours

Two Yuma police cars followed closely by an unmarked Ford Taurus speed by Emily's parked Explorer. None of the police officers notice Emily's hiding place nor expect that their phantom super sleuth is watching their pursuit of the child serial killer. Instead, they are fixated on serving an arrest warrant for Thomas Farrell, a man who has never held down a job for more than six months in his life, did not possess an arrest record, and who hasn't even received a parking ticket. This man was one of the most wanted killers in Yuma at the moment and nothing was going to compromise this arrest. Two more patrol cars and the forensic van rush to catch up with their colleagues.

Detective Rivas pursues his killer perp with absolute determination. He rushes the driveway, gun drawn, followed closely by three eager patrol officers and his rookie detective partner. The air is stifling and dusty causing a slight constriction in the pursing officers' throats. Perspiration has already begun to pour down the sides of the detective's face. His hands begin to feel the increasing moisture, but he squeezes the grip on his Glock even tighter.

He manages to command police identification at the front door, "Yuma Police Department!"

An instant later the detectives and officers burst through the entrance of the small rundown house. Loud voices are heard from inside with strict instructions to lie down on the ground. After a few moments everything stops. It is quiet and completely still as the stagnant air outside.

Detective Rivas is the first to exit the home with the child serial killer in handcuffs. Thomas Farrell, his head hung in front of him, seems like a weak pathetic man woken from a wonderful dream only to discover that his dream has turned into a nightmare. He never utters a word as he is quickly ushered into the back of a police car. The serial killing spree has finally ended.

The patrol car drives away and Detective Rivas

watches for a moment with so many questions racing in his mind.

John interrupts the detective's thoughts, "Is the house secure for my techs to begin the evidence search?"

"Absolutely. I want every inch of the Suburban gone over too. I mean everything. I don't want anything thrown out in court."

"You got it." John gears up for the long tedious task of collecting evidence.

Emily still continues to watch at a safe distance as the crime scene investigation unfolds; she is impressed by the lead detective's proficiency and integrity of the crime scene. She has witnessed many homicide investigations and the unpredictable investigative skill levels are inevitable with any type of police work.

Two patrol officers roll out yellow crime scene tape to block the neighborhood off to the curious and the news media. After the families have been contacted, the news media will report the newest serial killer to the public and it will become the topic of conversation for many weeks.

Evidence technicians are beginning to exit the basement carrying more than a dozen white five gallon buckets filled with evidence. The Suburban is scrutinized for fingerprints, blood, fibers, and any other organic and inorganic matters that can be identified. Detective Rivas is directing a technician to the types of photographs he wants taken.

Emily puts down her binoculars and takes a sip

of stale coffee. She knows that this crime scene work will take the officers and technicians most of the day to complete. She is satisfied with the results and the rest is up to the criminal justice system. With the public's zero tolerance for child molesters and murderers, justice should be swift and hopefully extremely painful for Thomas Farrell.

Now completely exhausted and fatigued, Emily backs the Explorer out of her vantage spot and slowly drives away from the crime scene feeling a sense of accomplishment and some deep sadness for the loss of innocent life.

A couple yards away from the crime scene tape, Detective Rivas notices the Explorer driving away. It's an unusually high-end vehicle for this particular poor neighborhood and he didn't notice it earlier. He's unable to get a complete license plate except for "N7" and the tinted windows block the identity of the driver. He files this incident in the back of his mind for now before returning to the crime scene.

* * * * *

Emily eases the Explorer onto the freeway heading west on Interstate 80 to California. Traffic moves smoothly, most cars are heading east into Yuma rather than west to California. In about nine hours she will be pulling into her own driveway. Taking a few deep breaths and pressing her aching back against her comfortable leather seat lumbar, Emily's mind focuses on being home instead of tracing the steps of a serial killer. She can't wait to take some much needed time off. She wondered if her parents would approve of her chosen life path. She remembers how wonderful summers were at age six going to the lake with her parents, swimming, and gathering as many river rocks as she could carry.

There were many wonderful years with her parents until that fateful night during the summer just before her twelfth birthday. If only her parents had driven or taken a taxi instead of walking home from the party, they would be alive today. The nice police detective had tried to explain to her that it was a random killing of a robbery gone bad and her parents didn't suffer. She remembered the tension in the police detective's voice when he explained what happened and how he held her hand in support. The murderer was never caught. After twenty years the thought of a murderer roaming the streets free to enjoy whatever life had to offer, made Emily outraged. The only consolation was that she had Uncle Jim in California who opened his home and life to her.

Emily settles back for the long drive ahead. Her BlackBerry vibrates and she glances at the screen. She programmed child abduction information in California to alert her. It was just updated information regarding an old case.

A mile behind Emily's Explorer, a new Chrysler Crossfire sports coupe increases speed to one hundred twenty miles per hour. The dark steel blue automobile punches the limit as the engine sings and glides over the road like glass. The vast unpopulated landscape of scrubby brush is a mere blur across the horizon. The feeling of pure power consumes the driver with absolute addiction.

Emily keeps glancing at her BlackBerry to see what other news and information is available. She takes her eyes off the road for no more than two seconds as the Crossfire appears out of nowhere and clips the Explorer's rear quarter panel. The hit and run vehicle is gone in only a couple of seconds, never slowing down as if it was a ghost from her past.

Emily grasps her steering wheel tightly and slightly overcompensates for the sideswipe intrusion. She loses control of her Explorer and begins to skid. The high-profile vehicle doesn't stand a chance to regain control of the road; it tumbles over and over several times before resting on it's smashed roof on the side of the freeway. The entire vehicle is crushed beyond recognition and Emily's high-tech equipment from inside the cab scattered in plastic fragments more than a hundred yards along the freeway. Heavy dust and debris filter thirty feet in the air above the still spinning wheels. Emily remains strapped in her seat, unconscious and bleeding. Her breathing becomes slow and shallow.

Chapter 5
Friday 0830 Hours

It's a typical California morning at Seascape beach with a heavy fog shelf hanging over the bay that will usually burn away by noon. The beach generally brings about fun in the surf and positive memories for most people, but for Detective Rick Lopez of the Santa Cruz County Sheriff's Office it brings dread.

The watch commander called Detective Lopez shortly before 0700 hours to report that an early morning jogger discovered the body of a young woman. It's officially the seventh homicide of the year, and it unfortunately won't be the last.

Detective Lopez has worked homicide for the past six years and for most of that time he has been the lead investigator. In his mind, very few police officers currently on duty at the Sheriff's Office would be qualified to run an efficient and competent murder investigation especially without an independent forensic unit. At least, not an investigation that would generate any promising leads and suspects outside the obvious cast of players. He's not looking forward to cleaning up the mess of this investigation because it has now already begun without him. Several patrol cars and an unmarked detective car are parked parallel along the street.

Detective Lopez parks in a quiet, coastal, suburban neighborhood of Aptos with a mere population of ten thousand. The beach is nowhere in sight, but the cool sea air hits his senses as he exits his vehicle. He grabs a notebook, clips his cell phone on his belt next to his Glock 19, and carries an extra police radio.

The crime scene is located at the end of a well-traveled dirt path approximately a quarter of a mile long that winds down to the sandy beach just underneath a train trestle. He's annoyed that patrol hasn't roped off the entrance to the path yet. It's a potential access and escape for the murderer and could possess any type of significant evidence: footprints, murder weapon, discarded beer can or cigarette butts. Now the evidence, if there was any, is most likely contaminated.

Detective Lopez begins his short hike down the beach access path through a thick grove of trees. It allows him to get his thoughts together before confronting his investigative team. Any other time it would have been enjoyable to jog down the path and take a nice long run on the beach. He makes quick notes of areas on the path that need to be given special attention and documentation; there are some discarded litter pieces that appear to be new and broken branches of bushes and overgrown foliage that could lead to potential footprints or drag marks of the crime.

As Detective Lopez approaches the beach, he hears voices. It was unmistakable to recognize the loud dialogue of his two crime scene detectives Matt Saunders and Ken Williams. They were like two identical frat boys delivering a punch line every time they answered a question.

There are several patrol officers meandering around the crime scene from fourth watch. Their shifts were already over and officers from the first watch should be taking over the security detail of the crime scene.

Detective Lopez approaches two officers drinking coffee and eating breakfast scones, "I need you to secure the entrance to the path."

The officers nod in agreement and begin to head up the path.

Stopping them, Detective Lopez says, "No I

need you to secure this area, you'll have to go around."

The younger patrol officer gapes at the detective, "Around?"

"That's what I said. You have a problem with that?"

"Uh no", the younger officer replies.

"Have you ever a secured a crime scene before?"

"Yes."

"Then I suggest you secure this one now."

The two patrol officers head down the sandy beach to the next set of stairs. It will take them a good fifteen minutes to hike to their location. They grumble to each other as they trudge through the heavy sand trying not to spill their coffee.

Detective Lopez directs another patrol officer to barricade off a large section of the beach for the crime scene area.

"Take a large section on both sides and keep everyone out." To other loitering police officers, "If you're not needed here, you can get back to your patrol duties."

"Hey detective." Matt approaches with a cynical look on his face. "You seen the broad yet?" He nervously bites at his index fingernail.

"Working my way over." Detective Lopez still surveys the beach area and the trail leading up to the street.

"She's a real beauty. Looks like the work of both an organized and disorganized offender." He clears his throat and looks for a compliment.

"That's not likely."

Ken joins the detective group. "The perp did a real number on her. What do you think?"

"I need you both to thoroughly identify and collect evidence including anything on the beach path."

Matt replies, "One step ahead of you. Found some bloody clothes and a credit card. Although the credit card belongs to a Herman Mellow and looks like it's been here for an eternity."

Detective Lopez continues, "Don't forget to photograph everything in place before collecting. No matter how trivial."

Ken smiles, "We're on it boss."

Matt takes overall photographs of the crime scene and begins closing the distance to the body. Ken starts to package the few pieces of evidence.

A few seagulls fly overhead and captures Detective Lopez's attention for a moment. Circling high above the rocks swoops a falcon, an impressive hunter, who relentlessly searches for smaller prey with powerful speed and extreme accuracy. In essence, the sea-dwelling bird is an extremely effective killing machine that leaves little room for error. The detective hopes that this isn't a sign of things to come.

Detective Lopez approaches the victim's final resting place. He pays particular attention to anything that appears unusual surrounding the body and becomes convinced that the victim was killed in another location.

The victim is a white female between twenty-five and thirty-five years old lying face down between the path and sand. She is partially clothed with only a pair of unzipped black jeans and a white bra. The bra had been twisted and hooked haphazardly like someone else dressed her in a hurry. Severe lacerated wounds are on the back of her neck and back, it has left an unusual tearing pattern. Her left shoulder blade shows a tattoo of a blue and yellow butterfly.

Matt joins Detective Lopez, "What do you make of her position? Posed?"

The body looks as if she was interrupted while praying and gives the appearance of a deliberate pose created by the killer.

Detective Lopez puts on latex gloves and begins to examine the body a little more closely, "She didn't die like this, but was put in this position. Staged. It looks like her final cause of death is strangulation though." He looks at the thin purplish marks around her neck.

Matt studies the body, "Does her arm look strange to you?"

Detective Lopez observes that her right arm at the shoulder has been severed. "It's a clean cut." He points to the hands, "But look, her fingers and fingernails are not the same."

"God, it's an arm from someone else? Talk about a definite signature." Matt ponders.

Standing up, Detective Lopez states, "I want everyone to spread out and see if we can find the arm that belongs to this victim and any other body parts. There could be other bodies." To Matt, "You're right it does look like the work of both an organized and disorganized offender."

Matt replies, "A serial killer?"

"Let's not get ahead of ourselves. We need to ID this victim immediately and conduct a complete victimology to try and find out where she might have met up with her killer. Start going through missing person reports while the coroner gets prints and a tox report."

Matt leaves, "I'm already way ahead of you. The coroner should be here any minute to transport the body."

Unfortunately, Detective Lopez fears the worst. Santa Cruz County has a serial killer on the loose and this is only the beginning of the body count. It hasn't been the first time Santa Cruz has witnessed the destruction left by a serial killer. Edmund Kemper and Richard Mullins terrorized the county during the 1970s. But what's even more disturbing, it looks like the work of two serial killers working together, one an organized offender and the other a disorganized offender. One serial killer is now training another serial killer.

Chapter 6
Friday 0900 Hours

Sparks fly sporadically in a brilliant artistic display as firefighters use the Jaws of Life to free Emily from her metal tomb. Four firefighters begin to peel back the crumpled metal as an ambulance waits to take her to the Yuma Regional Medical Center located ten miles away.

Emily fades in and out of consciousness still strapped upside-down in her driver's seat. She's vaguely aware of the rescue workers trying desperately to free her, but it seems more like a dream and everything is moving in a slow disjointed motion. Loud mechanical sounds and chemical smells are faint only in the far distance of her mind.

Firefighters operating in unison look like carnival workers with their bright yellow slickers. Traffic has slowly begun to back up in the westbound lanes. Emergency vehicles, police cars, and a tow truck block any through traffic until the rescue is complete.

Emily is extracted from her Explorer and safely put on a gurney. The dry heat of the day makes every life sustaining breath difficult. The blinding sunlight revives her for a moment as oxygen is administered directly into her lungs. Her mind races with intense anxiety as she remembers her computer equipment is still inside the wreckage and a loaded Beretta is strapped to her left ankle. Her true identity is at risk. Her life's work and the lives of children are in jeopardy. She tries to sit up and take control of her situation, but concerned voices calm her back down as she is loaded into the back of the ambulance.

* * * * *

The thirty-seven bed emergency medical center in Yuma has some of the most current state-of-the-art equipment and medical care for the Arizona area. Nurses and doctors move easily about the corridors to check on patients.

Emily has been considered extremely lucky and

didn't suffer any life threatening injuries or broken bones, just numerous lacerations and bruises. Hospital policy stipulates that she must remain under observation overnight. She is propped up in her hospital bed with fresh bandages on her arms and face. At least she can finally get some rest.

A young fair-haired nurse enters Emily's room. "How are you feeling?"

Letting out a sigh, "Much better, thanks."

"Would you like more water?"

"No thanks, I'm okay." Emily pauses, "Where are my things?"

The nurse motions to the other side of the room, "Over there."

"Actually, I was talking about my computer equipment."

"From inside the car?"

"Yes."

"Well I think it'll be towed to the wrecking yard for safe keeping with the car", she supplies the restroom with more soap.

"I need to make a police report about the hit and run driver."

"Don't worry about that now, the police will be interviewing you before you are discharged." She smiles and looks at Emily, "Just let me know if you need anything."

Emily nods and the nurse leaves the room. Sleep seems inevitable; Emily's eyelids feel increasingly heavy. The sedatives must be taking effect. There's nothing that she can do now except come up with an explanation of why she had several guns and high-tech equipment in her car. Hopefully, the police will be satisfied with her answers and not get curious about her visit to Arizona.

Chapter 7
Saturday 0900 Hours

High above the surf and rocky coastline in Seascape, the ultimate hunter-killer takes a thrill ride among the wind thermals with a carefree ease. The Peregrine Falcon's large but compact fourteen-inch body takes aim at smaller and less fortunate birds.

The falcon spots a small nesting California bird hiding in a crevice just inland from the beach. Turning its direction downward, the falcon begins the descent with a dramatic flair. It reaches a speed of more than one hundred miles per hour, strikes with deadly accuracy by ripping open the small bird's back and neck, and retrieves the victim with no difficulty. The dagger-like black claws finish the job.

It is a compulsive search for a specific victim; the most likely prey that will satisfy the intense fantasy created in the mind of the hunter. The Killer sits motionless in his Ford Truck and watches people enter and exit the shopping center grocery store and large department super store. They go about their day not knowing what lurks just around the corner. They never look around them to see who might be watching. They are intensely focused on where they are going next and not who could snuff out their very existence.

The Killer considers how it would be so satisfying to become a Peregrine Falcon. He takes a long deep breath trying to imagine what it would be like to be free. Life would be so much simpler, and he would command respect and even be adored for being such a great hunter. He has so much in common with the great sea-flying hunter here in Santa Cruz County. He continues to watch women leave the store with little interest; many are carrying bags filled with store sale items and various groceries.

The Killer has begun to move through the first phase of withdrawing from everyday activities, while becoming stronger and more alert to the daily atmosphere. He now moves into the second phase. Senses are heightened and the world appears more vivid and alive. The thrill of extinguishing vital energy and then consuming it entirely makes the man blink in anticipation as he sees a young brunette woman leaving the store carrying a small grocery bag. She seems unsure of herself by the way she carries her body across the parking lot, looking down at the ground. She gets into her blue Honda and backs out of her parking space never wise to the Ford Truck slipping in discreetly behind her.

The fantasy has begun to come to life with a living, breathing victim. Not for long. The trolling phase has shown him the plan and now he must wait for the exact moment to lure the victim to him. The Killer is one step closer to becoming one with the Peregrine Falcon and to eventually being free.

Chapter 8
Saturday 1130 Hours

Emily rests comfortably in her hospital bed with her eyes closed. It should be anytime that her discharge will be official and she can go home. In the meantime she has reserved a rental car until her insurance paperwork has taken effect and she can get a new car. However, her electronic equipment and firearms are another story.

Emily shifts her body slightly causing a shooting pain to travel from her lower back up to her neck. Her numerous cuts and bruises are minor inconveniences compared to the impact injuries to her back. She moans slightly and opens her eyes. A man is standing at the foot of her bed holding a small notebook watching her with curiosity. She blinks her eyes and focuses on the gun, holster, and badge.

Sitting up slowly, "What can I do for you officer?"

"Ms. Stone, I'm Detective Rivas with the Yuma County Sheriff's Office. I just have some follow up questions regarding the accident." He smiles.

"Sure, I don't remember much though." She stares at the detective and immediately recognizes him from the crime scene gravesites.

"Just tell me what you remember."

"I quickly looked down at my phone, and when I looked up, a dark blue sports car veered into my lane and clipped my quarter panel."

"Do you remember anything about the car? Make? Model?"

"It was a new car like a small Mazda, Toyota or one of the Chrysler coupes. It had a lot of chrome, I think." Emily tries hard to remember.

"License plate?"

"Sorry." She shakes her head.

Detective Rivas had his questions initially ready for her before walking into the hospital, but after seeing her in the hospital bed, he hesitates. He can't quite figure out why this beautiful woman had guns and high-tech equipment in the car and a Beretta strapped to her ankle.

Emily hides her nervousness during the awkward silence, "Detective?"

"What do you do for a living Ms. Stone?"

"Emily."

"Okay Emily." His attention wavers a bit.

"I'm a writer. I write mystery short stories and blogs on the Internet."

"There were two guns retrieved from your vehicle and one taken off your ankle in the emergency room." She never averts his gaze. "Can you explain to me why you need that much fire power?"

Emily smiles and pauses a moment knowing that the detective is watching her every move. She is petrified that he will find out who she is and what her real motives are for being in Arizona. Not to mention the email she sent him. She holds her voice and body language steady as she answers, "My research and travels take me to many places. I don't feel safe being a woman and traveling alone."

"I see." Detective Rivas is not sure if she's telling the truth, but he feels that she's definitely hiding something.

"I have permits for them, if that helps. Obviously, they were probably destroyed in the accident."

Detective Rivas looks at his notebook expecting something to tell him what to do next. "There were some computers and equipment that were salvaged from the accident scene."

"Oh." Emily didn't know what else to say. She waited for the detective to explain further.

"You can pick them up at the department's evidence impound along with your firearms."

"Thank you, that would be great."

A nurse walks into the room. "Excuse me, Emily you are discharged. I need you to sign some papers before you go."

Relieved, Emily answers, "Thank you."

The nurse leaves the room. Detective Rivas is satisfied for now, but again he mentally files this information.

"Is there anything else that you can remember about the crash or before?"

"I don't think so."

The detective gives Emily his business card, "Please feel free to call me if you remember anything else."

Taking the card, Emily says, "I will, thank you again detective."

Detective Rivas hesitates for a moment, but decides to leave. "We have your current contact information?"

"Yes."

"Hope you feel better soon." He leaves the room.

Emily exhales in relief. She knows that the detective suspected something. She doesn't care now and slowly gets out of bed and begins to get her things together. Her limbs feel overworked and tender. She can't wait to get back on the road again and get home. This time hopefully without incident.

Chapter 9
Saturday 1900 Hours

The dingy bar with antique tables and stools hosts plenty of people who are blowing off steam from their busy week. Lively conversations resonate at the bar, laughter is heard over carefree conversations, and beer flows freely. Three young college students are playing darts. The bar maid chats with patrons as she moves her stocky frame in between tables.

At a corner table directly underneath some black and white historical prints of California, sit the two crime scene detectives. Matt lifts his dark amber ale and appears annoyed as he speaks in low tones to his partner Ken.

"It's simply amazing that Rick is such a tight ass. Talk about a power trip." Matt slurs his words slightly after four tall glasses of beer.

Ken picks at his Coors label and listens to his partner.

"Doesn't it just make you nuts?"

Ken looks up from his bottle, "It is what it is."

"Ah man, you know exactly what I'm talking about." He gulps some ale. "Working hard on a homicide where no one gives a shit. She wasn't a victim. It's like taking out the trash."

"It could be viewed that way."

"It's such bullshit in this town. You could easily get away with a homicide."

"What do you mean?"

"Look, most people who commit homicides are careless and stupid." He looks around at the patrons. "You just have to plan carefully."

Taking a sip of beer, "Why are you so adamant about this?"

Leaning forward, Matt continues, "You really think that we're going to find out who killed that bitch at the beach? Huh?"

"Well, I'd like to think that we would at least try."

Matt leans back in his chair looking like he has already said too much. He shakes his head in disgust and waves the waitress over to the table. "Can we have another round?"

Ken watches his partner. He's not always cared for his crudity, but he knows that he's always got his back.

Leaning forward and speaking softly, Matt says, "Doesn't Rick's higher than thou attitude get to you?"

"I just ignore him. But he's a good cop."

"Maybe."

Ken laughs.

Matt rants on, "All I'm saying is there are people who just aren't worth the time and energy in a homicide investigation."

"And who is supposed to pick and choose? The rich, the politicians, the government, or just plain hard working Joe Blow?" Ken chuckles.

The waitress brings another round to the detectives.

To waitress, "Thanks." To Ken, "Aren't you sick and tired of busting your ass for the dregs of society?"

"It's what we do."

Matt leans back, "Yeah well things are going to change. In fact, things are already beginning to change." Obviously too intoxicated to drive, he watches a couple of young women fumble at the bar and order another drink.

Chapter 10
Sunday 1200 Hours

Trees and perfectly manicured flowerbeds bursting with a rainbow of pastel colors surround a small two-story tan home with dark driftwood trim and a large deck above the garage. Pine and Eucalyptus trees cast shade and privacy from the neighborhood homes and closely surround the property.

Emily pulls her rental white Jeep Liberty into the driveway and turns off the engine. She sits in her car for a moment and takes a deep breath. Still feeling the motion of the road and the stinging aches of her body, she slowly opens the car door. She's anxious to get safely inside her home away from the callous reality of serial killers. But first decides to go to her neighbor's house across the street.

The lovely manicured yard strikes an almost melancholy chord with Emily. It reminds her of when she was a young girl growing up in Indiana. Her parents always had a beautiful garden and wonderfully colored plants hanging around a patio with white wicker furniture. She can almost smell the fragrance of the flowers and air of springtime. Her memories are interrupted by an incessant barking, then followed by a large jet-black Labrador retriever bounding towards her.

"Sergeant, hey boy!" Emily drops to her knees and pets the big brute. "I missed you so much." Uncontrollable licks to the face are her punishment for being gone.

Theresa Brandon, an attractive middle-aged woman with short grey hair, appears from the back yard wearing pale yellow cropped pants and t-shirt. She quickly takes off her gardening gloves to greet Emily. "I thought that was you."

Emily looks up, "Hi Terry."

Theresa sees the cuts on Emily's beautiful face, "Oh your face. You said that you were in an accident, but I had no idea."

"It looks much worse than it really is."

"Come inside and sit for a bit. I made some iced tea."

Smiling, Emily agrees, "That sounds great."

Sergeant follows Emily and Theresa into the house. Through the threshold, it opens into a spacious living and kitchen area with glass windows from top to bottom and a front row seat to the sixteenth fairway. The vibrant natural greens are pleasing to the eye and immediately relax your body and psyche. Emily loves to sit and stare out at the vast green fairway watching the golfers hunt for their stray balls.

Theresa pours two glasses of iced tea and gives Sergeant fresh water. "Are you going to be able to salvage your car?"

"No, I'm afraid not. I've got a rental until I can get a new car."

Giving Emily a tall glass of iced tea, "Are you sure you're okay?"

"I'm fine." She smiles reassuringly and tastes her iced tea, "It was a hit and run. I was just in the wrong place at the wrong time."

"You know you didn't have to rush right back. We love taking care of Sergeant. He's such a little angel."

Sergeant perks his ears and tilts his head to one side.

"Thank you, but it's really nice to be home."

Taking a sip, "Did you get your research done?"

"Pretty much." Emily hates lying to her friends, but it's the way it has to be in order to ensure her anonymity and safety. The Brandons think she's a writer and does work for various companies online.

"Mmm, this is great iced tea and the lemons are from your garden." Emily asks.

"You know me too well."

Emily leans back on the comfortable sofa, "What's been going on here, anything exciting?"

Theresa becomes a little quiet, "Well I didn't want to burden you with this right now."

"What?" Emily's interest is now piqued.

"Someone has moved into the house next door to you."

Smiling, she says, "What is it a family with six kids and twelve dogs?"

"No, I wish it was that simple."

Concerned, Emily asks, "What's the matter?"

Theresa explains, "It's just one man. He's been causing a problem in the neighborhood."

"How much trouble can he have caused? I've only been gone two weeks." Emily is concerned because her friend isn't the type to exaggerate, so it must be serious.

"He does some kind of tree work and has been trying to get neighbors to use his services." Theresa pauses before continuing, "Emily he's been threatening some of the older residents and they're scared. They don't want to call the police because they are afraid of retaliation."

"Who is this guy?"

"I know this sounds kind of crazy, but that's exactly what this guy is – crazy. He behavior is very erratic and bizarre."

Emily is upset that anyone would try to scare

her neighbors, "Sounds like he needs an attitude adjustment."

"Oh Emily, stay clear from this guy. I have a bad feeling about him."

Emily says reassuringly, "Don't worry, I'll be fine."

The door to the garage opens and an energetic middle-aged man wearing glasses appears. "Hey, she's home."

"Hi Robert."

"Thought maybe Sergeant might not remember you." He teases.

Theresa laughs, "Fat chance of that."

Sergeant is curled up at Emily's feet, content and softly snoring, happy that she's home.

Pouring himself a glass of iced tea, "Did you tell Emily about her new neighbor?"

"I was just filling her in."

"He sounds like he doesn't take his meds very often." Emily tries to make light of the situation.

"I have to agree with Terry, you be careful." He continues.

Emily takes a couple of sips of her iced tea and looks outside, watching a father instruct his son on his golf swing. "He's just a bully, and we'll just have to see how long he'll last around here."

Chapter 11
Tuesday 0800 Hours

The early morning fog casts a dreamy mist over the neighborhood. The backyard is filled with blooming annuals that frame the pine trees and wild ferns. There is an Acacia tree bursting with yellow blossoms between the two houses and a pale yellow dust covers the fence.

Emily opens the sliding door and steps out onto the deck with Sergeant at her side. He hasn't wanted to leave Emily's side since she has been home. She sips a steaming cup of coffee as she gazes out in the yard. Something catches her attention along the fence line. Quickly, Emily slips on a pair of shoes and treads down the back stairs to investigate.

As Emily nears the fence, she realizes that one of the branches from her new neighbor's side has damaged the fence, particularly her side. It appears that the branch was deliberately cut and left on her side of the fence. It was unbelievable that her new neighbor was trying to force his tree cutting services on her by deliberately cutting a branch down. He's going to be sorely mistaken if he thinks that Emily is going to fall for his scam. She wasn't going to let this man extort money from her.

Before Emily turns to go back into her house, she hears a noise from the other side of the fence. She stops and listens. The noise seems to stop as she strains to listen. What was this guy doing? Emily decides to exit her gate leaving Sergeant behind and goes over to her neighbor's house to find out what's going on.

Before she steps onto the property next door, a man appears out of the trees and stops directly in her path. The stocky man with dark hair and a well-trimmed beard looks more like a timber man from the mountains. His hair, neatly trimmed in a bowl style hides his eyebrows and draws attention to his dark beady eyes. His pale face and dark features bore into Emily like a predatory animal.

Caught slightly off guard, Emily maintains her stance and authority, "Hi, I'm Emily. I was just coming over to talk to you about that branch on the fence."

"What branch?" He quickly retaliates in an accusatory tone.

Calmly, Emily states, "The branch that is sitting on the fence."

"What are you talking about? You come over here to accuse me of a branch on the fence." He stands up straighter to give the appearance of power, but his slouchy sweat pants and flannel shirt say otherwise.

Emily begins to see what her neighbors were telling her about this man. She smiles in disbelief, "Look, it's not a big deal, but I'd appreciate it if you could get that branch off the fence before there is any more damage."

"What's wrong with your face?"

"Excuse me?"

"Why are you looking at me like that?"

Emily decides to play along with this man's paranoid game, "Like what?"

"You know what you're doing."

"I'm a reasonable person, but I'd appreciate, at your convenience, if you would remove that branch from the fence."

"That branch has damaged a wheelbarrow and golf cart."

Emily is amazed how this man can spin a story, "So you do know something about that branch you left on the fence?"

The man begins to makes fists and releases them

several times; it is obvious that he's beginning to fume over this situation that's not going the usual way he planned. Emily isn't impressed or intimidated by his words or actions and he painfully knows it.

"I can sue you for the damage." His voice raises an octave in pitch.

"Go ahead, but in the meantime please remove the branch." She smiles, "Nice to meet you."

Emily turns and walks away. This conversation is like talking to a brick wall with a psychopathic attitude. She closes the gate in her back yard. Before she reaches her sliding door, she hears a terrible crash from inside her neighbor's house. A voice booms from inside followed by several more crashes. Emily could only make out a few words and she definitely heard her name spoken in the midst of ranting madness.

Chapter 12

Tuesday 1400 Hours

Paso Robles is a coastal mountain city located just twenty-five miles from the Pacific Ocean on Highways 101 and 46. It is more specifically known as the "Pass of the Oaks" and home to more than twenty California wineries. Thirty thousand residents call this growing, diverse town their home.

A car slowly moves along El Camino Real and turns down several side streets watching for pedestrians. The middle school has just let out and children are walking home, while others are boarding yellow buses and jumping into mom's SUVs. One Sheriff's deputy patrol car is parked at the entrance to the school. The car continues to merge with other traffic without drawing any attention.

Children laugh and talk as they walk down the streets. But Susie Williams walks alone staring down at the sidewalk. She's unsure about her path and walks with trepid steps. Her long blond hair is pulled back in a ponytail fastened with a neon pink barrette. She carries a Disney backpack loaded with schoolbooks and her empty lunch box. She only looks up for an instant and crosses the street away from the crowd of children.

The car turns down the same road as Susie. It pulls to the side of the road, and stops. The man synchronizes his watch to the exact time of day and makes brief notes in a small pocket sized steno pad pulled from his top pocket. Susie walks on continuing home.

Chapter 13
Wednesday 0230 Hours

Emily is sound asleep in her comfortable king size four-poster bed. She rolls over to her side enjoying a pleasant relaxing dream without serial killers. Sergeant is snoozing in his cozy doggie bed in the corner of the bedroom. His ears suddenly perk up and his sleepy eyes open. It's dark and quiet, but something has awakened him because of his keen senses. He stealthily gets up from his warm bed and exits the bedroom. He stands quiet, statue-like in the hallway, eyes alert and scanning every corner. His eyes have completely adjusted to the darkness, but he still remains motionless.

Sergeant moves to the spare bedroom and stands at the threshold listening; it's just a guest bedroom with an open closet door. The closet seems to pique his interest. He moves toward it. As soon as he moves his large head in the direction of the closet opening, it slams shut forcing him inside the closet. The door latches and something heavy is placed in front of it. He begins barking incessantly and uses his large paws to try and shred the frame around the door.

Emily opens her eyes awakened by Sergeant's barking and scratching. Before she can roll over and sit up, a dark figure restrains her and a jagged hunting knife presses up against her neck. Emily blinks to focus her eyes on the figure breathing in her face. His knee is against her ribs, it's extremely painful since her bruises from the accident haven't healed yet.

The dark figure wears a ski mask disguising his identity. He leans into Emily and whispers, "Kak kak kak." He waits a moment and then repeats, "Kak kak kak."

Emily thought that she didn't hear him correctly; he seems to be speaking gibberish. Her mind races to who this person is and how Sergeant is confined. There must be someone else in the house too, but she can't be sure. Her mind is reeling and her heart is pounding. The adrenaline is pumping at an all time high urging her to make a move. Otherwise, she won't have a chance to stay alive.

Again the intruder leans in, but this time he whispers, "You're going to die. You can't escape."

The intruder shifts his weight slightly, letting some of the pressure off of Emily. She doesn't waste any time and makes her move, using a sucker punch to the intruder's upper stomach with her right elbow. As he flops to one side in agony gasping for air, Emily has just enough time to leap out of bed dressed only in a tank top and panties. She knocks over an antique plant stand that is used as a clever hiding place for one of her handguns. She doesn't have to waste any time loading the weapon, since there's already a clip of fifteen rounds armed and ready.

Before Emily can turn around in a shooting stance, a stained glass lamp from her nightstand flies through the air and makes contact with her shoulder. It crashes against the wall and shards of multi-colored glass shower the room. Emily is momentarily stunned as an excruciating pain radiates through her right arm down to her fingertips. She drops the gun. Making a quick alternative choice of weapon, she grabs a small wrought iron chair and swings it wildly, striking her assailant on the side of head. He goes down. She scrambles for her gun as her wrought iron chair hurtles through the sliding door barely missing her head by inches. There is so much glass in her bedroom that you can't see the color of the carpet anymore.

Emily can hear Sergeant barking relentlessly

from the other room because he can't get to her aid. Before she can stand up with her gun, she's struck on the back of the head with a heavy blow. The room spins in one direction and sounds become strangely muffled. Slowly she collapses on the floor. She sees a pair of police issue boots standing next to her. She fights the darkness that's gradually creeping into her peripheral vision, but her eyelids can't hold up the horrendous weight anymore. Sound and light disappear as Emily falls into an unconscious rest. The gun drops onto the floor next to her crumpled body.

Chapter 14
Wednesday 0300 Hours

A small grungy bar in Seacliff just a stones throw from the beach has been closed for about an hour. There are still local patrons leaving the establishment staggering out to a taxi, while others opt to walk home a few blocks away. It's quiet and still with a lingering scent of the foggy bay.

Ken sits in his unmarked police vehicle and watches the last few regulars leave the bar. He reflects on what his partner said about how getting away with a crime in Santa Cruz County would be simple. Where did his cynicism come from? He agreed with his partner about how easy it would be to get away with crimes nowadays, but they still had an important job to do nonetheless. They had to perform their duties as best as they could.

Ken knows exactly how crimes, homicides in particular, are investigated. He knows all the little loopholes and tricks to find a suspect. He finds and processes the evidence from these crime scenes. That's what his job entails; no one questions him about methods or integrity on the job. What a perfect cover, especially with the thin blue line of silence to back him up.

He observes two young women leaving the bar; they yell something back to the bartender and giggle to one another. The two women sway and stumble as they walk down the sidewalk and then disappear around the corner. Ken makes a mental note of the description of the two women and the direction of their home. He rubs the side of his temple with his fingertips and tries to ignore the splitting headache pounding inside his skull.

Chapter 15
Wednesday 0315 Hours

The dark abyss of disorganized swimming thoughts and memories floats erratically in and out of her mind. Struggling to get to the murky surface of reason seems near to impossible. Suddenly there is surge of water pushing from side to side making it difficult to stay afloat.

Emily slowly becomes aware of her surroundings as Sergeant licks and nuzzles her face with his wet nose. She can feel the carpet underneath her cheek. She blinks quickly; each time she feels a shooting pain up the back of her head. Sitting up, Emily steadies herself as the room slows its nauseating revolutions. Sergeant whines and sits down next to her as if to say everything's okay.

"Hey boy, you okay?" Emily runs her hands over the sleek flat coat searching for any type of injury. "How'd they get an upper hand on you?"

Sergeant appears to be fine, the only blood Emily finds is her own from a minor cut. She gets to her feet and spots her gun still lying on the floor. She begins to run all of the previous events through her mind, weighing the scenarios of the possible suspect or suspects.

Pulling on a pair of jeans and sweatshirt and nursing her aching head, she tucks the gun in her waistband and begins to investigate her home for any clue to the identity of the perpetrators.

The doors and windows are secure, except the sliding door in her bedroom. Even the front door is locked. The spare bedroom had a small writing desk propped up against the closet. Sergeant had splintered the doorframe and pushed the desk slightly forward to make his escape. Nothing was moved in the house and nothing appeared to be stolen. This meant that the invasion was solely to intimidate, hurt or kill her. The intruder could have killed her if he chose to, but instead left the house and locked the door behind him.

Emily opens the front door and steps out on the porch. She listens. There's just silence. She half expected several police cars to come screaming up with sirens blazing with the whole neighborhood watching the events unfold out their windows. But there was nothing; homes were dark and still. Her neighbors must still be sound asleep and unaware of the attack. It would have been a different story if there were gunshots fired. She would have quite a bit of explaining to do. Calling the police at this point would be senseless; there's little if any real evidence that would help to catch the intruder. The cops might get curious about her or dig up something that she didn't want to have to explain.

The whole situation didn't sit well with Emily. The entire time, about ten years, that she's lived in this neighborhood nothing has happened. Not even a burglary or domestic violence. She contemplates and weighs the odds of the situation and what has changed recently. Her thoughts keep coming back to one probable suspect – her new neighbor.

Chapter 16
Thursday 1000 Hours

The small one-room Sheriff's substation office is located in the shopping center for easy community access. There are just four desks, some locking filing cabinets, and a unisex restroom. Most people merely walk by the office on their way to the grocery or hardware stores, never taking the time or interest in the local police department. When there was a police officer inside, they are usually writing an incident report, taking a break chatting with another officer, or using the restroom.

Emily sits in her rental Jeep observing two uniform deputies and a plainclothes detective through the two large plate glass windows of the substation office. She contemplates her next move and really doesn't look forward to interacting with the local police. It's too close for comfort. She knew that she needed to report the new neighbor's activities for her neighbors' sakes, but not her recent attack. No doubt that this new neighbor will have a criminal record, and then it will be easier to get him to move – he's only renting the house.

Emily found out from the Brandens that his name is Donald Everett. She quickly checks her makeup in the rearview mirror, hoping that her cuts and bruises appear minimal. She tells herself that her makeup is as good as it's going to get under the conditions and puts her sunglasses away.

Emily unconsciously lets out a big sigh as she gets out of her car. She walks to the door of the substation office and it opens before she can grasp the doorknob. Two uniformed deputies, one really tall and thin and the other muscular, stare at Emily. They dramatically move out of the way and allow her to enter the office. The two deputies continue out the door to their patrol car, but not before comments to one another were made about Emily's appearance.

Emily ignores the two police officers and moves towards the seated detective. She observes that he is studying what appears to be homicide photos and miscellaneous reports, most likely witness reports.

She had read in the newspaper about the woman found on the beach and realized that he must be a homicide detective. It seems strange that he was stationed at the community service substation and not at the main county building located in downtown Santa Cruz.

Detective Rick Lopez continues to study his reports and doesn't look up. Emily notices that he is actually quite attractive with dark hair and green eyes. He's fit and muscular, but has a brooding demeanor that keeps people at a distance. He's casually dressed in a black polo shirt and slacks instead of a dress shirt and tie.

Emily interrupts the detective's thoughts. "Excuse me."

Detective Lopez didn't look up immediately, which annoyed Emily. No wonder people don't like to talk to the police, she thought.

"What can I do for you?" The detective shuffles the graphic homicide photos into a neat stack placing a manila folder on top of them to hide them from view.

"I would like to report a problem in my neighborhood."

The detective finally looks Emily in the eye and holds her gaze. He can't help but notice that she a beautiful woman with intense eyes. Immediately, his thoughts are curious about the cuts on her face. "He states, "Domestic?"

"What? No." Emily is beginning to get really bothered by the lack of interest. "I would like to report a person that has been harassing and threatening elderly people in my neighborhood."

Detective Lopez relaxes a bit and leans back in his chair. He studies Emily with some interest. "Please have a seat."

Emily looks around and finds an uncomfortable metal chair on the other side of the room, drags it over to the detective's desk, and sits down across from him. She feels conspicuous and uncomfortable.

The detective takes out a legal yellow steno pad. "What's your name?"

"Emily Stone."

"Address?"

"This is about the guy who just moved in next door to me."

The detective asks again, "Your address?"

"529 Spruce Drive. The new neighbor's address is 527 and his name is Donald Everett." Emily watches the detective write down some notes on the steno pad in tiny printing at the bottom of the page.

"Do you want to file a report?"

"He hasn't done anything to me. But my neighbors are mostly retired and they are afraid of him and don't want any kind of retaliation." Emily continues, "He tries to get them to use his tree trimming and landscape service and when they refuse, he threatens them. I think this guy is capable of real violence if given half a chance."

The detective pauses and studies Emily carefully; he feels that she is truthful but not telling everything. "What would you like us to do? Talk to him?"

Emily realizes that she's wasting her time. She says, "Look, this guy shows signs of potential violence and he behaves erratically. Might be because he's on meds or he's just psychopathic. Can you just contact the home owner about their renter?"

"I'll look into it. But if he's harassing people or threatening violence, they need to file a report with the Sheriff's Department. Or dial 911."

"Fine. Thanks." Emily felt that her concern had fallen on deaf ears and that she had only been talking to herself. She gets up from the chair, "I'll let you get back to your homicide." She leaves the office without waiting for a response from the detective.

Detective Lopez watched her get into the Jeep, pull out of the parking place, and disappear into traffic. He thought it was interesting that she caught he was working on a homicide case. He couldn't get her intense dark eyes out of his mind long after she left the office.

* * * * *

Detective Lopez refers to the Psychopathy Check List to assist him in creating a threshold assessment of his serial killer. He knows that serial killers are generally psychopathic and are unemotional, egocentric, lack remorse and empathy, deceitful and manipulative, and posses early behavior problems and adult antisocial behaviors. Well that sums up half of the population, he thought dryly.

The threshold assessment is used as an investigative tool that incorporates the initial physical evidence of behavior, victimlogy, and crime scene characteristics. Many detectives simply go by the nearest person to the victim and work the case accordingly, but with serial cases, it must be methodically connected in the investigation. Detective Lopez studies behaviors and homicide crime scenes whenever he has the chance to help strengthen his knowledge of crime scenes.

When it's quiet with very little interruptions at the substation, Detective Lopez can put some of his best thoughts together about a homicide case. He knows several things so far about his beach victim. She has been identified as Candace Reynolds, a thirty-six year old who worked at the local coffee shop a couple days a week, with no boyfriend, and a family who lives in Portland, Oregon. Additionally, she had an elevated blood alcohol level.

The body was posed at the crime scene showing control and a grandiose tendency by the organized killer; he feeds on recognition and control. The body was sexually assaulted and killed in another location. Both killers brought the body to the beach, knowing that she would be discovered in a short period of time. The cause of death was strangulation and the severe lacerations on her neck and back were inflicted post mortem as was the arm amputation. The coroner said that the cut could've been done by a small chainsaw or another type of electrical cutter, but not removed by a knife.

Candace's friends and coworkers said she liked to walk to the local bar in the evenings and walk home at night. No one the night she died said she left with anyone or noticed anything unusual.

Even though this homicide hasn't been officially considered a serial crime, Detective Lopez knew that it was only a matter of time. The killer must've studied her routine and found out the best time to interact with her without any possible witnesses. His best guess was the walk to and from the bar. A neighbor? Another bar patron? The killer has average to above average intelligence, is manipulative, works a non-skilled job such as the service industry, and has enough impulse control to lure his victim into a false sense of security before he strikes.

What Detective Lopez wrestles with is the fact that the crime scene looked like it was committed by two serial killers. Who would seek a serial killer teacher? As he contemplates the types of individuals who would be drawn to this killer and why, his thoughts drift back to Emily Stone. He can't seem to get her out of his mind. And he's beginning to feel a little bit guilty for not giving her his full attention.

The detective clicks through several programs on his laptop and types in Donald Everett in the criminal justice data base with an approximate age between thirty and forty years old. He waits. Several individuals come up on the screen, most are over the age of fifty-five. He zeroes in on one, Donald Christian Everett. He was born in San Jose, California and is thirty-five years old. His previous residences are numerous.

There were more than a two hundred complaints in the past six months for assault, harassment, stalking, minor drug possessions, and miscellaneous civil lawsuits. This guy had quite a history; Detective Lopez decides that he's going to find out more about him.

Chapter 17
Thursday 1200 Hours

The restless nights have become drawn out and nearly unbearable with each passing hour. Every time he closes his eyes, the mind begins to roll its own movie of the perfect victim, each time with even more crystal-clear intensity. It stirs the intense compulsion deep within his soul to seek another victim and to sustain their life only until their last breath completely consumes him, only then is he ultimately free.

The severed arm is safe in a heavy plastic bag in

a freezer. It's important to have something from the last kill to bring to the next. All victims have been connected through him and with each other. They will ultimately bring him the freedom that he so desperately seeks. To be free with the falcon. To hunt as the falcon. And to take a victim as the falcon.

The Hunter-Killer watches with even more intense interest as he drives through town, only stopping once in a while to observe the habits of potential victims going about their day. The victim must meet the criteria that have been designated by the endless killing fantasy. The ferocity continues to build deep inside his soul making it difficult to think about anything else such as eating or sleeping. The compulsive drive keeps him moving forward until the last possible moment of the trap. The thought makes him excited and barely able to contain his violence. The lure and capture will be soon – tonight.

Chapter 18
Thursday 1330 Hours

Detective Rick Lopez pulls into Emily's driveway and parks behind her white Jeep Liberty. He leaves his detail sheets in the car, but grabs a small pocket notebook. He exits the car and scrutinizes the entire neighborhood within view. He could see why Emily was concerned; the neighborhood was almost picture perfect with beautifully landscaped front yards, freshly painted modest homes, and an abundance of wildlife fluttering in the many surrounding trees. The worst thing that could happen on this street would be to have a psycho move in and disrupt the balance and tranquility of everyday life.

Rick is completely sold on the neighborhood because of the eighteen-hole golf course that meanders through several of the connecting streets. He would like to move in right now, but unfortunately his police salary wouldn't cover the mortgage in this neighborhood. He walks up to the front door and knocks. He waits. No one answers. Emily's car is parked in the driveway. Maybe she's in the shower, at a neighbor's house, or on the phone? He retrieves a business card and was just about to slip it through the door.

The sound of a muffled groan interrupts Rick's thoughts. He stops. He hears the faint mutters again. It sounded like it was coming from around the back of the house. Instinctively, Rick moves to investigate. He walks around the house and carefully flips the gate latch entering the backyard. He stops and listens again. The noise becomes louder and it appears to be the voices of two people. There is a distinct pounding sound of a heavy impact followed by a distressing voice. The detective unfastens his gun holster and retrieves his weapon. He moves forward to a plain wooden door. He takes a moment and grasps the doorknob. Not taking another moment to think, he flings the door wide open.

A large man in a mesh tank top is holding Emily in a front chokehold. Both look startled by the detective's entrance. The room has been con-verted into a small training gym with punching pads for boxing, a weight bench, and several mis-cellaneous free weights.

"Detective?" Emily blinks a couple of times, not really believing that the detective is standing at her door holding his police issue firearm on her.

The buff man releases Emily and takes a step toward the detective. "Can I help you?"

Interrupting, Emily says, "Leo it's okay, this is a police detective." She takes off her wrist wraps.

Rick looks at Leo. "Leo?" He reholsters his gun.

Shoving his large hand in front of the detective, the man introduces himself, "Leo Lewinski."

Slowly, "Detective Rick Lopez." He shakes the man's hand.

Emily giggles, "You thought that I was being at-tacked?"

"Well it..."

Emily continues, "Leo is my personal trainer, sometimes a bit unorthodox in his training methods, but he helps me to be able to defend myself and stay in shape."

"I see." Rick feels really stupid and tries to re-cover gracefully.

"What brings you here?" Emily enjoys watching the detective recover with his pride barely intact.

"I wanted to follow up on your report."

"Give me a moment?"

"Sure, no problem." He takes a step back and appears to be interested in the backyard.

Leo stands close to the detective during the entire conversation like a watchdog. Rick can't help but take an immediate dislike to the personal trainer with his see through tank top and tanning studio tan. He seems shifty and overcompensates with an alpha male dominating personality.

Emily discusses a few techniques with Leo and then sets up another appointment.

"Thanks Leo, see you tomorrow morning."

Leo leaves, but not before he says with a definite sneer, "Nice to meet you detective."

To the detective, "Come on up." Emily opens the interior door to the downstairs area. A large black dog bounds through the doorway and jumps on the detective. "Sergeant, off!"

Rick runs his hands through the fur on the large dog's neck. "Hey there Sergeant." He loves big dogs and this one was a prize.

"I think he likes you detective."

Rick follows Emily up the stairs to the living room. He notices the sliding door in the bedroom has been taped up with cardboard where the window has been smashed out. As he walks up the stairs, the detective sees that it was a nice view of the trees.

Emily goes to the kitchen and takes a bottle of cold water out of the refrigerator. "What can I get you detective? Mineral water, juice, diet soda? Sorry I don't have any coffee made."

"Mineral water is great, thanks." He watches Emily move freely about the kitchen looking for a glass. He muses that she is very attractive dressed in her black running pants and pink jog bra. He notices that her cell phone is clipped to her waist.

Sergeant takes his spot next to the sliding door where he can watch everything that goes on in several rooms.

"Here you go detective." Emily hands Rick a tall glass of mineral water and directs him to the living room. She sits down on the couch sipping her water.

Rick feels a bit uncomfortable now sitting alone with Emily in her house. He begins, "First, I want to apologize for my behavior earlier. I didn't want to give you the impression that I didn't care about your complaint."

Emily is amused by the detective's apology. "Well, I have to admit, I wasn't very hopeful that the police were going to do anything."

"I pulled up some information about your neighbor and he seems to cause serious problems everywhere he goes."

"Especially with his weird behavior."

"He has several drug related arrests. It's something that the Sheriff's office can bust him for, and then that would get him evicted from your neighborhood." He takes a drink of the mineral water. "And your neighbors won't have to get involved. Everybody wins."

Emily's cell phone tones an alert. She quickly glances at the screen and becomes distracted. The detective observes an immediate change in her demeanor.

"Do you have to be somewhere?"

"No, it's just email stuff." Emily becomes pre-occupied with her hands.

"What do you do? For work?" He never takes his eyes from hers.

"I'm a writer. I write mystery stories and blogs on the Internet."

"I see." Rick has the strong feeling that Emily's not telling the complete truth and her deception makes her nervous. "So you work at home?"

"Yes." She motions to a small den off the dining room.

"Is there anything else you want to tell me?" The detective is often masterful at manipulating people to telling him more that they want to tell.

Emily's phone tones again. "No, just that there's a nut that lives next door." She smiles.

"Okay. I'll see what I can do and contact narcotics." He retrieves a business card and gives it to Emily. "Call me if you have any more information or," he pauses, "any questions."

Taking the business card, she adds lightly, "Thank you detective. And thanks for coming to my rescue."

"From what I saw, you don't look like you need any assistance."

Rick gets back inside his car and turns the ignition key. He glances up the second story windows and sees Emily watching him leave. He can't help but think that there's more going on than what meets the eye.

Chapter 19
Thursday 1430 Hours

Emily watches the detective drive away and gazes out the window after he's long out of sight. She's not sure if his visit was for her complaint or something else. The detective seems legitimate and shows integrity about his work. Her immediate racing thoughts go directly to her anonymity as a serial killer hunter. Does he know? Will he find out? She pushes her negative thoughts to the back of her mind for now.

Emily's immediate concern was the alert on her

BlackBerry displaying the California Amber Alert that a seven-year-old girl has been abducted in Paso Robles. She goes to her small home office to gather all the information available.

The room resembles a high-tech command center instead of an average home office. Sitting off to the side, there are several phone lines with voice modifiers. Underneath one of the desks is a cleverly hidden drawer that houses another Glock, easy access for any type of emergency. The room has been painted in a soothing light blue with two landscape photographs to soften the sterile equipment harshness.

There are two worktables that are pushed up against one another with three computers constantly running with wireless technology. It doesn't include her mobile laptop. Now she has to purchase another one, since her last one was smashed into a billion pieces on Interstate 80.

Emily begins to search all available news breaking information on the Internet regarding the abducted girl. She uncovers that the girl, Susie Williams, was taken on her short walk home from school. Emily pulls up maps from Google and Mapquest to assist her in the location and distances between the school, home, malls, and parks, in addition to the pedophiles living within the areas. The girl is described as petite, blonde, blue-eyed, and small for her age. She was a perfect victim for a trolling, pedophile, serial killer.

Retrieving maps and miscellaneous information,

Compulsion

Emily adeptly uses the computer technology to her advantage by educating herself on the limitations. She also accesses the crime statistics in the Paso Robles area as well as any information from San Louis Obispo County that takes many of the surrounding cities into consideration. In addition, there are many hiding places to keep a child, commit murder, and dump the body without the local authorities ever knowing where to look.

Emily has gone to great lengths to update herself with computer technology, limitations of the criminal justice field, and child serial killer profiling. She uses every resource available on the Internet. Slowly a new plan begins to emerge to track this killer. This time she remains obsessed to find the child alive. She has a backup plan to retrieve even more information. She picks up the phone and dials.

* * * * *

Valparaiso, Indiana is a bedroom community where crime is relatively uncommon and not tolerated by the citizens. Children play in the streets and wave to passing cars. Neighbors look out for one another and help out whenever they can. Most residents do what's right, even in a world where greed and materialism is rampant. Valparaiso is a true neighborly town and that's the way people like it. And that's the way it will stay.

An unpretentious home complete with a manicured lawn and a white picket fence is the object of concern. A Porter County Sheriff's Office patrol car pulls up to the driveway where there is already another patrol car parked out front.

Sergeant Mike Sullivan gets out of his patrol car to assist one of his officers. He hoists his short stocky frame up the driveway, removes his sunglasses revealing a slight red tan on his fair skin. His uniform hasn't been professionally ironed, rather he tried personally to flatten the creases the best he could with an iron that was on the fritz.

Deputy Palmer greets the sergeant before he reaches the top of the driveway. "Sir, we've been trying, but no luck."

"Well, let me give it a try." He follows the deputy to the front door.

A tiny blue-haired elderly woman is patiently waiting for the officers. She states good heartedly, "I see you've brought in backup."

"Yes, ma'am." The sergeant moves to the living room window where the screen has already been removed. He begins to jimmy the window and with a little luck and precision, the window pops open.

"All right sergeant!" The deputy exclaims in admiration.

"Oh thank you officer. I'm such a ninny when I went out and forgot my house key. And I don't want the brownies to burn."

"Not at all ma'am. It's my pleasure." The sergeant heaves himself clumsily into the window and disappears inside the house.

A few seconds later, the front door opens and

the sergeant appears. "I've saved the brownies and turned the oven off."

"You boys come inside, I'll serve you up some of those brownies." The woman steps inside the house not waiting for them to follow.

The sergeant answers as he pats his round stomach, "I don't mind if I do." His cell phone rings and he looks at the number. He motions to the deputy, "I've got to get this; you go on ahead. I'll be right there."

After the elderly woman and Deputy Palmer are inside the house, Sergeant Sullivan flips open the cell phone, "Hey stranger." He listens carefully and looks at his watch. "No problem, give me two hours to get that information, and I'll call you back. It's good to hear from you. Talk to you in a few." He closes his cell phone and goes inside the house to get that homemade brownie.

Chapter 20
Thursday 2300 Hours

The Ford Truck creeps slowly into the Manresa Bar and Pool Hall parking lot and finds an out of the way location underneath a pine tree. The headlights and engine cut out, but an occupant remains behind the wheel obscured by the tinted windshield. The truck, dressed with a camper shell to conceal what's in the back, doesn't draw any particular attention to any of the patrons coming and going.

The out of the way bar and pool hall is a favorite for many locals and tourists in the Seascape area.

It's a great place to meet friends and relax from a busy day. Groups can be seen chatting and laughing as they leave the establishment.

The Killer gets out of the truck and moves toward a 1992 beige Toyota Celica. He tries the door; it's unlocked. With a quick swipe of his hand, he unlatches the hood release. Moving expertly, like a predatory animal, he lifts the hood and disengages the distributor connection. He closes the hood with little noise and returns to his truck to wait. The Killer knows that it's only a matter of time before his next victim walks out of the bar.

Her schedule was extremely predictable; she rarely changed her routine and tonight was no exception. She awakes at six thirty every morning and showers, leaves for work by seven thirty usually eating a walnut muffin and drinking a cup of coffee as she backs out of her driveway. After work at the flower shop, usually five twenty, she goes home to her duplex to feed her cat and leaves again by seven thirty to arrive at the Manresa Bar. Her life has made a full circle and now he will have to set her free so that he can absorb her existence.

The Killer lights a cigarette and leans against his car causally waiting for her to leave. He didn't have to wait long, barely a whole smoked cigarette.

The thirty-one year old brunette exits through the door of the bar, digging her keys out of her purse. Taking a couple of seconds, she retrieves the key set careful not to chip her fuchsia nail polish. She opens the door to her Celica and plops down in the seat. The ignition turns on, but the car winds down not able to achieve a spark to start the engine.

The Killer approaches the woman, "Hi. You need a jump?"

She scrutinizes the man for a moment and smiles, "Thanks. That would be great."

"I've got some tools in back of the truck. It may take me a moment to find the jumper cables."

She gets out of her car relieved that someone is going to help her and she won't have to call the auto club. "No problem, I'll give you a hand."

They walk to the truck together. She looks him over and lets her guard down. He looked wholesome enough to her.

She asks, "After you get my car started, can I buy you a drink?"

The Killer smiles, "Sure."

He stands for a moment at the back of the truck. He flips up the back window and opens the tailgate. The interior is dark.

"Looks like you need a flashlight." She leans in to the back of the truck and strains her eyes to see.

A fist from inside the camper jabs her face with two quick successions. Her nose and lip are instantly bloodied and she slowly falls backward to the Killer, unconscious. He gently lifts her into the truck cab and the Accomplice pulls her into the darkness.

The excitement of the capture has electrified the Killer almost into a rampage frenzy as he gets behind the wheel, barely able to contain his anticipation of the kill.

Compulsion

* * * * *

A rural section of Watsonville accommodates many sizable ranches that raise horses, cattle, goats, and sheep. The truck eases up an unmarked dirt road off of Larkin Valley Road. The headlights dim and then switch off, but the truck continues to move forward to a barbwire fence.

The fence has a rotten post, and the strung wire easily moves aside to facilitate entry. Tall dried weeds and oak trees are abundant, giving the ideal cover. No one would ever see the two Killers performing their work, and the victim will be found after the morning sun rises.

The Killer gets out of the truck and opens the tailgate. His Accomplice appears from the back, dragging the awake and terrified woman. She has common duct tape over her mouth that also binds her hands and feet. Her eyes are wide with unimaginable fright, her body language pleading. The Killers continue to their work as if it was a well rehearsed play, never hurrying or unsure of their next move.

The Accomplice drags the woman through the fence to an open clearing and leaves her there for a moment. Both the Killer and the Accomplice synchronize their watches; it is ten minutes before the stroke of midnight. It is perfect timing; the last breath must be exhaled exactly at midnight.

The Accomplice tears the woman's clothes from her body and throws them aside. He begins to violate her sexually until his fury is satisfied ignoring her whimpers and moans. His fingers proficiently wrap around her thin throat squeezing until she passes out, she briefly regains consciousness several times, and then he squeezes even harder.

The Killer takes a plastic bag from inside the cab of the truck and brings the severed arm to meet the air before it will eventually take refuge in its final resting place. He walks to where the Accomplice has just finished snuffing out her life. Now, it's his turn; he will leave his mark and merge the once lively essence to his own. He will leave the mark of his alter ego on the back and neck of the victim. He's that much closer to becoming liberated from the world and being free.

Chapter 21
Friday 0700 Hours

Before he leaves, Rick locks the front door to his modest two-bedroom house. Carrying a medium sized suitcase and duffle bag, he walks to his unmarked police vehicle, opens the back door and tosses his luggage in on the back seat. After slamming the door shut, he looks back at his house where his wife watches expressionless from the living room window.

It's finally gotten to this point where he's moving out and going to stay at a weekly motel in town.

He has no doubt that this is the beginning of the end, which will ultimately be divorce. He knew that he couldn't make a daughter of successful doctor happy on his salary. She has never been happy being a cop's wife; it was too tough for her. There's nothing that he could've done to make things better, she's just not happy. For once, he's glad that they didn't have any children because they would suffer the most.

Rick gets in behind the driver's seat and stares out at his neighborhood for a moment. He thinks fondly of his nice neighbors. His cell phone rings conveniently interrupting his current woes.

Pushing the receive button, he barks, "Lopez." He listens for a moment, "I'm on my way." He hangs up the phone. It's just as he expected. There's been another homicide.

Chapter 22
Friday 0730 Hours

Emily packs the last piece of electronic equipment in the back of her rental Jeep. She is annoyed by the fact that there's quite a bit less room than her Explorer, but it'll just have to do. Sergeant stays close to her side, hoping that he might get to come along this time. He sits down and stares directly at Emily.

Feeling a bit guilty, Emily explains to the dog, "I'm just going to be gone for a few days." Sergeant just looks at her. "You always have a great time with them. I promise I'll bring you something special."

Emily picks up a grocery bag filled with individual dog food servings and treats. Sergeant obediently follows her to her neighbor's house.

Theresa opens the front door before Emily has a chance to knock. "Thank you so much for looking after him on such short notice", she says.

"Don't think anything about it; we love Sergeant. It gives me someone else to talk to." Theresa opens the door wider and Sergeants pads inside.

Handing Theresa the bag, "Here's some more food and treats. Thanks again. If you need anything else feel free to get it from the house."

"Bye. Be careful."

Emily returns to her Jeep and seats herself behind the wheel. Her mind is reeling from the information she's gathered about the abducted little girl. Her first stop will be Paso Robles and the exact location of the abduction. She will then finalize her plan of visiting the specific locations and narrow the list of suspects. As she finalizes her plan in her mind, she drives up the street to the main road.

A truck almost cuts Emily off; Leo takes the turn with considerable speed barely missing Emily's Jeep. He slams on the brakes and rolls down the window.

Surprised, Leo says, "Hey Em where are you going? I thought we had an appointment this morning?"

"I'm so sorry Leo I forgot; something came up.

I'm going to be out of town for a few days."

"No biggee. I've got another appointment close by."

"I'll call you to reschedule when I get back."

He smiles showing one of his shiny gold teeth, "No problem. Catch you later."

"Bye."

Emily eases up her electric window and drives on.

She looks in her rearview mirror and watches Leo take the turn down her street and disappear out of sight. With the monotony of the road, her thoughts return to the missing little girl. If she doesn't make any stops, she should arrive in Paso Robles in two hours.

Chapter 23
Friday 0800 Hours

Rick doesn't have any trouble finding the crime scene. There are many emergency vehicles already there with both marked and unmarked police cars parked along Larkin Valley Road. The detective finds an available space a little distance from the dirt road entrance to the crime scene. There's nothing like a grisly crime scene to take his mind off of his impending divorce. He exits his vehicle.

A uniformed deputy approaches the detective, "Detective, the scene is a ways up the dirt road, and we've secured the entrance and the crime scene until you arrived."

Rick was pleasantly surprised that this young deputy was thorough and eager to work. He couldn't remember his name. The detective looked at his nametag: Monahan. "Thanks Monahan. You first on the scene?"

"Yes sir. I received a call from the property owner that he found the body."

"Have you interviewed the owner?"

The deputy looked at his notebook and said, "Yes, he has about sixty surrounding acres and was checking for broken fences early this morning when he discovered the body."

The officers began walking up the dirt road, which was evidently used for additional access to the property for utilities or livestock. Rick regards the entire area in order to get a feeling for why the killer would choose this exact location. It was rural with native wildlife, and no one would see him doing his killing. There was something else that bothered the detective. The killer obviously wanted the body to be found. But how did he know that the body would be found today? Maybe he didn't. This might prove to work in favor of the investigation.

The crime scene detectives Rick and Ken had recently arrived at the scene and were already talking loudly and joking with other officers about the crime scene. Detective Lopez ignored the inappropriate comments for a moment while he continued to assess the scene.

Deputy Monahan explained, "It looks like there were tire tracks up to the fence, but they were deliberately destroyed." He continued, "It looks like he used a shovel and possibly a rake by the way the dirt is pushed aside with these marks."

Rick studies the loose dirt and agrees with the deputy's assessment. "Good work Monahan."

The deputy smiles at the detective with renewed confidence.

As Matt approached Rick, he said, "The part time crime scene photographer they just hired last week called in sick today. What do you want to do?"

Rick looks around for Deputy Monahan and spots him talking with another deputy. "Deputy Monahan."

The deputy jogs back over to the detective. "Yes detective."

"You any good with a digital camera?"

"Absolutely."

"I want you to take photos of the crime scene and surrounding areas. Take overall photos, then medium distance and close up shots depicting the scene. Can you handle it?"

The young deputy is thrilled to be a part of the crime scene investigation of a serial killer. "Yes sir."

The detective gives the deputy his keys. "There's a digital camera with an extra battery on the floor of the back seat of my car."

The deputy takes the keys, "I'm on it." He leaves.

Matt says, "Well now that's settled." He shows

the detective the body. "It's been staged. It's like the perp is trying to mock us in some perverted way." He explains further, "I've never seen anything like this."

Rick carefully enters the crime scene area through the broken barbwire fence and notices that there is what appears to be blood and maybe fabric on some of the sharp twists of barbwire. "Make sure that Deputy Monahan gets photos of this Matt." The detective gestures to the potential evidence.

"No prob." Matt continues on to an open clearing beside a tree.

Rick stops dead in his tracks and takes in the killer's demonstration. He has personally walked more than sixty homicide crime scenes, but nothing has prepared him for this presentation. It made him think of a Hollywood movie that has been presented over the top with a horrifying and dramatic display of serial killer victims. He thought that this scene would rival Hollywood's depiction.

The thirty-something woman is completely nude and propped up in a sitting position with her right arm tied above her head. The thin rope is then affixed to the tree. Her legs are neatly folded underneath her body. Her left arm is completely missing; a haphazard cut through her shoulder joint leaves a grotesque opening. Her head is bowed where her face is obscured. Even more disturbing is the arm that lies across her lap. She appears to be gazing down at it.

Matt interjects, "There's no doubt that we have a

serial killer huh?"

Ken joins the conversation, "A preliminary search of the crime scene didn't reveal any clothing, purse, or identification of the vic."

"Keep looking", Detective Lopez instructs. "There's more evidence here than meets the eye."

Deputy Monahan takes photos of the body and moves closer to get photos of the rope, knots, and severed arm.

Rick realizes that keeping this crime scene from the public is going to be almost impossible. To the crowd of officers, "Alright everybody listen up. No one comes in or out of this crime scene unless I say so. And nobody speaks to the press or the public. That's means friends, family, girlfriends, spouses, whatever. Understand?" The crew responds with nods and continues to perform their duties.

Rick approaches the body careful not to disturb any evidence and looks closely at the type of rope used and the severed arm. He was sure that this arm was from the last victim, but he'd have to wait until the medical examiner turned in his report. There was the same tearing on the back of the neck and upper shoulder area as the previous victim. The woman appears to have been dead longer than eight hours.

He definitely knows that this killing was the work of two killers because there are too many conflicting behavior patterns. One distinct pattern was the need to make an elaborate display, where the killer spent quite a bit of time with the victim before and after the actual death. He posed her and even cleaned some of the blood from the gaping wounds. It was almost like making an art project for a gallery display. This individual wants recognition, something that he feels that he's never gotten and now he's found an outlet that will give him just the notoriety that he craves.

The other killer was extremely erratic and frantic about his contribution to the crime scene; often making the scene more disorganized by his inconsistent behavior. He wants something that's more personal and even Biblical in his mind. He's more of a traditional serial killer, if there's such a thing, and feels that his victims give him the much needed power in his quest for supremacy.

Rick takes in depth notes and sketches of the crime scene as Ken and Matt process available evidence. As the crime scene investigation continues, it becomes obvious that it's only a matter of time before the killers' strike again, depositing this victim's arm at another crime scene. It was going to be a race between the cunning killers and the determined police.

Rick re-evaluates the overall crime scene and evidence before releasing the body to the coroner's office. He watches a couple of autopsy technicians cut down the body and load her into a body bag. They carefully package the severed arm in a small heavy plastic bag for transport.

The pieces of the serial murder puzzle are waiting for a resolution and are screaming to be deciphered. Rick struggles with his instincts and the politics of the local county government. The processed evidence must be couriered to the San Jose Crime Lab to be properly identified for DNA and any matching samples for when a suspect is identified. The detective wonders if the two killers will be two friends that decided to kill for fun and games; or, will it be two people who met by accident and found out they have the same morbid interest in killing.

Chapter 24
Friday 1045 Hours

E mily pulls off Highway 101 onto Sixteenth Street in Paso Robles. She would have been there sooner, but she chose to stop for gas and to grab a quick bite to eat. She stocked her car with drinks and high protein snacks in case she got a promising lead right away. Then she won't have to worry about missing a meal. Riding shotgun next to her is a new laptop computer, running with a wireless Internet access ready for any search that she might need.

It's a bright, sunny day and under any other circumstances it would have been a nice day to visit one of the greatest wine growing areas in the United States. Paso Robles is a continually growing community that offers a variety of growth potential.

Emily keeps her focus on the street that little Susie Williams was abducted from. She didn't have to search long to find where the little girl disappeared. Banners, toys, photos, and flyers state that they wish her safe return home soon and that they love her. Emily clocked the distance from the school to her home, and it's barely three quarters of a mile. Houses were sparse in this neighborhood compared to the more populated areas in other directions. There would be fewer children walking in this particular direction and more opportunity for a pedophile to strike without being witnessed.

Emily pulls over to the side of the road to use her laptop computer and compare notes on the previously registered sex offenders in a twenty mile radius who prefer children, specifically young female children. She also had a list from a law enforcement database, thanks to her friend and confidant Sergeant Mike Sullivan in Indiana. Her first search with certain detailed parameters comes up with more than twenty possible suspects. As she narrows her search, three prominent suspects emerge. The three suspects are all in different cities of Paso Robles, Santa Maria, and Morro Bay.

The first suspect works at a grocery store in Paso Robles. Emily turns her Jeep around and heads in the direction of the grocery store and then the home residence of her first suspect to see if he's visible and track his movements before dismissing him altogether.

Chapter 25
Friday 1445 Hours

One of the least favorite job duties for Detective Lopez is visiting the morgue to view an autopsy of a homicide victim. The only thing worse is if the victim is a child. The Santa Cruz County building stands alone in the downtown area. Below all of the typical county offices is the morgue, a small compact quarters that houses the dead.

Rick sets off to the macabre space known as the "tombs" to see what his second serial homicide victim has to say. He has known the medical examiner,

Doctor Todd Grainger, for ten years and is amazed by how he can carve bodies up, remove vital organs for study, and still able to keep a great sense of humor about life. Working homicide investigations has definitely made an impact in Rick's own life. He sees the world as more of a violent and destructive place. What people are capable of doing to another person sickens him.

The distinct smell of cleaning agents hits Rick's senses immediately. He grimaces, swallows hard, and proceeds. He sees Doctor Grainger with an autopsy technician working on his case. The doctor is dressed casually and doesn't resemble a typical medical examiner with his baggy pants and bright yellow deck shoes. His long blonde hair is pulled back in a tight braid that falls down his back. He's upbeat and performs his duties seamlessly.

The newest victim is now cleaned up and laying on a stainless slab. The visual inspection has been underway. Blood and other fluids had been drawn for testing, and the body X-rayed, weighed, photographed, and measured. Trace evidence is of forensic importance in a homicide case. Head and pubic hair is combed for any vital evidence transferred from killer to victim. In this case, transferred from killers to victim. The hands had been carefully bagged for any possible evidence from her killers. The autopsy tech is scrapping her nails for any flake of skin or foreign matter that would identify a suspect. Afterwards, the body will be fingerprinted to assist in identification.

Doctor Grainger looks up, "Ah, the detective who likes to bring me jigsaw puzzle homicide victims."

Solemnly, Rick responds, "Any medical examiner can have an ordinary homicide. I thought I'd shake things up a bit."

"Indeed."

"What do you have for me?" The detective looks away from the body as his stomach tightens.

"Both homicide victims died due to strangulation and their larynx crushed with quite a bit of force. They had been strangled just enough for them to pass out many times before their actual demise. And their arms were removed after death."

"Sexual assault?"

"Yes, same as the first. The rape kit is being sent along with the trace evidence to the San Jose Forensic Lab." He adjusts his glasses, "You know the routine; should take a week or more."

The doctor begins the internal examination with a "Y" incision down the front of the torso.

Rick grimaces, "Anything unusual I should know about?"

"Except the fact that you've got a really sick asshole out there killing women and taking their arms? No, nothing. I'll have a report for you ASAP." He begins to open the chest for examination starting with the lungs, throat, esophagus, trachea, and upper spine. His assessment is methodical and scientific based on his extensive experience.

"Thanks Todd." The detective turns to leave almost in a panic.

"Oh detective?"

Rick stops and turns.

"The first severed arm?"

"Yes what about it?"

"It was roughly frozen for more than six months before it was left at the crime scene."

"Six months?" The detective's mind begins to process other homicides in the past and missing persons. "We haven't had any homicides missing an arm."

"That's precisely my point. There's most likely a body or parts of a body still frozen somewhere."

Detective Lopez reflects, "Another homicide victim."

"Bingo." The doctor is now emptying a thick sticky sludge of stomach contents into a stainless bowl.

"Thanks." The detective turns to leave as quickly as possible before the doctor begins removing more organs.

There's not much for Rick to do now, but hope that the forensic evidence will demonstrate some significance in the investigation. Matt and Ken are canvassing both areas in hopes of turning up any eyewitnesses who might have seen a suspicious car or van around the crime scene. He doesn't have much hope and his frustration is building. He feels completely helpless in this investigation because he knows that it's only a matter of time until there's another victim. The killers may be stalking their new victim right now. That thought discourages the detective. He tries hard to push the negative thoughts from his mind; instead, his thoughts turn to Emily and her nuisance neighbor. He decides to go to narcotics and coordinate a sweep of the neighbor's house.

Chapter 26
Friday 1600 Hours

After Emily dismissed her first possible pedophile suspect, she headed south on Highway 101 and then cut west on Highway 46 to the coast, and then south along the coastal highway to Morro Bay.

Morro Bay is a beautiful coastal community housing barely ten thousand residents along the historic coastal road of Highway 1 in California. Crime is not something this community endures, it is more reminiscent of some of the larger surrounding cities.

It is best known for its one hundred seventy-six meters high volcanic plug called the Morro Rock. It is home to one of the largest bird sanctuary and estuary in the state. Tourists visit this quaint community to view this prominent Rock and to dine at one of the many seafood restaurants along the esplanade.

One of the last known residences of her number two pedophile suspect is a farm in the Cayucos area just north of Morro Bay. It's rural and very sparse in population. Most of all, it would be a perfect place to keep a child captive and then dispose of the body without anyone ever knowing.

Timothy Dunne, age thirty-seven, wasn't a registered sex offender, but had many priors for indecent exposure, loitering, trespass, and committing lascivious acts with minors. He had been seen in other surrounding cities hanging around schoolyards and community parks watching children mostly under the age of ten. He had held countless odd jobs over the past fifteen years: handyman, carpenter, and deliveryman. His recently deceased parents had left him a small rundown house on twenty acres.

It didn't take Emily long to find out using a computer search everything about Timothy Dunne from where he went to High School, his divorce in 1998, and that he currently takes several medications for antisocial personality disorder and depression. She gets his date of birth, address, and vehicle license plate off the small subcompact parked in front of the house.

Compulsion

Emily finds an ideal parking spot camouflaged by trees on an adjacent property to the dilapidated little farm. She spies through a pair of binoculars and sees Timothy, who has Susie Williams with him. The child appears to be unharmed and not restrained in any way, but that could change at any moment. She watches the man pace back and forth as the child sits expressionless at a dining table staring straight ahead.

To Emily's relief, she's found the little girl alive and well. She types quickly on her laptop computer to alert the San Louis Obispo Sheriff's Office Emergency Services Division with all of the pertinent perp information, including a photo of Susie Williams. She hits the enter key and the information will be received on every patrol car laptop instantly without tracing back to her. It will lead patrol and detectives right to the farm to rescue Susie.

It takes every ounce of strength for Emily not to storm the house, pump six bullets into the pedophile's heart, and rescue the little girl. Just once, Emily would like to bring the missing child home to her parents personally. But for her work to be most effective, her anonymity is paramount. It's exceedingly lonely at times, but it's the way it has to be for her. In case the serial pedophile decides to run or harm the little girl, she sits and waits for the local authorities to respond.

The house is in an unincorporated area and it depends on where the police are located when a call comes in to them. It could take anywhere between ten minutes up to an hour for response. Emily continues to watch the house. Without warning, Timothy bursts out his front door onto the porch carrying a shotgun in his right hand. He has a crazed look in his eyes. He looks to the right, to the left, and then back to the right again. Obviously, he has forgotten to take one of his medications. His paranoid behavior has begun to show and his patience is wearing thin. Emily worries that he might hurt or kill Susie before the police arrive.

Putting down the binoculars, Emily inserts a full clip into her Glock. She gets out of the Jeep and looks down at the farmhouse, but she can't see where Timothy has gone. She frantically looks through binoculars and can't locate him. He's not inside the house, and he's not out on the porch or in the front yard.

Emily has completely lost a visual on her dangerous pedophile suspect. With her gun in hand, she begins to tread down the steep embankment and eases her way towards the farmhouse for a closer inspection.

Chapter 27
Friday 1615 Hours

Rick knocks for a second time on Emily's front door, but there's still no answer. Her car isn't in the driveway, but he thinks that maybe she has parked her Jeep in the garage. As he looks around the neighborhood he sees Theresa Branden through the picture window of the living room across the street. He decides to go and to talk to her about the new neighbor.

The detective looks at his watch and estimates that the narcotics team will be making their bold appearance in less than an hour. He walks up to the neighbor's inviting front porch with hanging pink fuchsias and knocks. Instantly a deep dog bark rumbles through the entranceway. A large black canine face appears in the picture window. He immediately recognized the doggie face as Emily's dog.

The front door opens and a middle-aged woman asks, "May I help you?" She then sees his badge and gun.

The detective hands her his card. "I'm Detective Rick Lopez with the Santa Cruz Sheriff's Office. May I talk to you for a few minutes?"

Theresa takes the business card and replies, "Please detective, come in."

The detective follows her, "Thank you."

Sergeant trots by the detective's side as he heads for the living room.

Theresa continues, "I'm Theresa Brandon."

"Nice to meet you."

"Please have a seat."

They both sit down. Theresa waits to hear what the detective has to say. Sergeant sits down next to the detective's feet.

The detective begins, "Your neighbor Emily Stone came to me to report the activities of your new neighbor."

"Oh." Theresa is somewhat surprised, but pleased.

"And I wanted to get some more information from you and your perceptions on the situation."

Theresa was happy to convey information. "This man is very unpredictable. He has intimidated some of the neighbors to pay him for services that he didn't do or was asked to do."

"Do you feel that he is dangerous?"

"Yes." Theresa gets her thoughts together. "I can't really tell you exactly why except for some of his actions towards others, but it's a gut feeling."

The detective appreciates her honesty. "I know about gut feelings."

Theresa smiles. "I bet you do."

The detective gets more information from Theresa about the neighbor in order to corroborate Emily's version.

Rick looks at his watch. "There is going to be a group of narcotic detectives visiting your neighbor's house in about a half hour." He continues, "I noticed that his truck was there. Hopefully, the narcotic detectives will find drugs and that will get him out of your neighborhood for good."

"That would be great."

"The landlord will have to evict him and the tenant will not have any legal actions against him because of the drugs."

Sergeant sits up and wills the detective to pet his ears.

Theresa laughs, "He likes you detective."

Petting the dog, "We've already met." The detective hesitates, "Well, I think that's everything I need. Thank you for your time Mrs. Brandon."

Standing up, she says, "Anytime."

They walk to the front door with Sergeant in tow.

"Do you know when Emily will be back?"

Theresa answers, "To tell you the truth, she said she was going to be gone for a couple of days, but sometimes it can be a week or more."

"Can you get in touch with her?"

"I have her cell phone number. She usually checks in daily to see how Sergeant is doing, but I don't expect her back until next week."

"Okay, thanks."

The detective leaves. Theresa was left wondering if the detective was more interested in the neighbor problem or Emily.

Chapter 28
Friday 1645 Hours

Emily eases her body closer to the farmhouse in a crouching position down the steep hillside, but she still can't get a visual on the pedophile. There are thick bushes and sharp thorns on some of the undergrowth catching on her jeans and scratching the inside of her forearms.

She loses her footing and tumbles a few feet, but a stout bush abruptly stops her descent. Her Glock sticks in the bush and she hastily recovers the weapon. She's covered in thick dust and has skinned her left palm trying to stop the fall. Blood begins to seep through the wounds. She stops and listens attentively, but she is stumped as to where the man went. He couldn't have gone far because he wouldn't have left the little girl alone.

Emily decides to climb back up to her car and get another vantage position. A bad feeling begins to creep into her body that she can't seem to shake. It's not anxiety, but rather a real feeling of danger. Her throat becomes dry and constricted, and her pulse elevates. She climbs faster; it's only another few feet to the top.

Emily runs practically into the barrel of a shotgun held by Timothy. He stands above her with careful aim and Emily knows he is prepared to use the weapon. Somehow he knew that she was watching him from the neighbor's property. She thought that she was so careful and confident about her position and surveillance approach.

He motions the gun at her, "Drop the weapon." His voice was absolutely expressionless.

Emily gets to her feet, a bit unsteadily, and drops the handgun on the ground.

He continues and gestures, "Move."

Emily obliges and moves slowly toward the wooded area, but her instinct tells her that he's most likely going to kill her and bury her body on the property somewhere. No one even knows that she is out here, and the police would never suspect that there's a body on the property.

She takes the opportunity to pretend to stumble

in a hole on the dirt path.

Timothy is annoyed by her unsteadiness and raises his voice now, "Get up! Move it now!"

"I'm trying", Emily whines.

Emily trips and goes down on the ground. She's on her hands and knees in a basically vulnerable position by most untrained observers. She glances up at Timothy and catches him taking the shotgun off of her for a moment. She then makes her move.

Emily rushes Timothy and body slams him against the ground. He hits the terrain hard, stunned by Emily's bold move, and tries to regain his breath. The shotgun clatters towards the hillside and briefly disappears out of sight.

Emily is briefly dazed as well. The impact of the hit made her teeth clack together causing a jarring insult to her head. A shooting pain penetrates through her frontal lobe causing an instant migraine. The minor cuts on her hands and arms are stinging, making her whole body buzz with a strange energy. She makes a move for her gun, but before she reaches the top of the hillside Timothy grabs her right ankle and yanks her away from the weapon. Emily hits the dirt again, but this time Timothy pins her down with his weight and wraps his hands around her neck.

"Die bitch!" He screams in her face with an absolute crazed look in his eyes.

Emily screams and scratches at Timothy's face. She's able to move her right knee up enough and slam it against his groin. Timothy drops to the side in searing pain. Emily gasps for air unconsciously rubbing her neck. She quickly gets to her feet and takes a fighting stance in case Timothy tries to attack again.

The sound of several cars entering the dirt driveway down below temporarily interrupt the fight. Both Emily and Timothy look in the direction of the farmhouse and see three police patrol cars skidding to a stop.

Emily begins to panic; she can't be found on the property by the police. Her cover would be blown forever and her life would be nothing but a nightmare of news media intrusions and do-gooders wanting her to solve many types of cases. It would never end.

Timothy takes another shot at Emily. This time, he's able to knock her off the steep hillside. Emily disappears over the edge.

Chapter 29
Friday 1700 Hours

Rick steps out of his parked car and meets with the crew of the Sheriff's Office Narcotics Squad. They meet on a street away from the intended location of Emily's neighbor. The narcotics sergeant meets the detective and provides a hearty handshake.

"Hey detective, nice of you to throw some work our way." He takes a step back with his hands on his hips.

Sergeant Dan Field stands about six foot six

inches tall and is almost twice the age of his young crew of four. Rick has known Sergeant Field since he first joined the department and has tremendous respect for him. He has collared many drug dealers and has served the department well in special weapons and tactics.

"I thought this delicate situation had your name written all over it." Rick jokes.

Sergeant Field asks, "What's up with this guy? His name keeps coming up on the radar."

"Not sure, but he's got no business here in this neighborhood harassing everyone." The detective continues, "He's showing violent and erratic behavior. There's no doubt that he has drugs in his house."

"He was picked up for drugs a few years back."

"Exactly."

Sergeant Field looks the detective in the eye, "So whose the wit?"

"What do you mean?"

"The wit, the good looking female that's got you all over this little sting operation."

The detective hesitates, "I wouldn't say."

"I knew it." The sergeant laughs. "Don't worry about it; we'll get this asshole out of this neighborhood. He'll be out by sundown tomorrow." He gives some specific instructions to his crew. To the detective, "Is he home?"

"Yes, his truck is still there as of ten minutes ago."

"Good. Come join the fun." To his crew, "Let's go."

Rick and the narcotics team assemble, get into their designated vehicles, and drive straight to Donald Everett's house.

The three vehicles pulling up haphazardly, make a clear-cut statement and block the driveway. Sergeant Field followed by two of his team, march up to the front door. He hammers loudly with his fist. "Mr. Everett, open up." He waits impatiently. He bangs again, "Open up."

The group hears some pounding noises coming from inside the house. Rick looks up at the deck. The filthy slider opens a few inches. The detective squints his eyes to see if Donald is peering out at the team. The slider suddenly bangs open and a stocky bearded man wearing old burgundy sweats and a long sleeved blue plaid shirt steps out onto the deck.

Donald fumes, "What do you want?"

Sergeant Field takes a step away from the front door and asks, "Mr. Everett?"

"I'm going to ask you again, what do you want?"

"Mr. Everett can you step outside please? We need to talk to you." The sergeant asks politely.

"If you don't leave immediately, I will have to report your unethical and illegal activities to your superior." He paces back and forth. "I've been minding my own business, but that neighbor has been disrupting my life." He gestures to Emily's house.

Rick is speechless by the Donald's strange behavior. If he had any doubt as to Emily's story of this man, he's completely behind her and the whole neighborhood now.

Sergeant Field pushes, "Sir, we can't talk to you when you're up there. Can you please come down to talk to us?"

Donald huffs and continues to pace, "I know my rights, and you have no business being here on my property without a warrant." He clenches and un-clenches his fists down at his side. He hesitates for a moment and then goes back inside, slamming the slider behind him.

Sergeant Field looks at the detective. "There's nothing more that we can do. He's right; he's spooky, but right." He takes a few steps down the driveway and looks up at the house. The shabby curtains are pulled tight. There's a crashing sound as if some dishes had been thrown inside the house. Then silence.

"I'm sorry for wasting your time." Rick tries hard not to show his disappointment.

"Don't worry about it, we'll keep him under surveillance. And I'll talk to patrol. We'll work some thing out."

The sergeant and his eager crew get back into their vehicle and leave the property. Rick opens his car door and looks back at Donald's house. He thought he saw the curtains drop back into place. There's something strange going on with Donald Everett thought the detective. He couldn't help but feel that something bad was going to happen.

Chapter 30
Friday 1715 Hours

E mily falls twenty feet down the embankment and is abruptly stopped by a dead tree stump. The dust slowly rises into the air. Emily coughs repeatedly trying desperately to free her lungs from the dry floating soil. She glances up to the top of the hill expecting Timothy to fire bullets down on her at any moment.

To her surprise, the shotgun is only a few feet from her. She almost forgot that the gun went down the hill during the struggle. She carefully scales to the left of the embankment and picks up the shotgun swiftly checking the chamber to see that there are two bullets ready for action.

Voices are heard echoing up the hillside from the farmhouse. The police have found the little girl and are actively looking for her captor. The law enforcement personnel spread out and aggressively search for the man who snatched Susie on her way home from school. They are not going to stop until they have this man in custody. Voices are becoming louder by the minute.

Both relieved and terrified, Emily moves horizontally along the hillside. Her mouth is dry and fine grit is embedded in her teeth, causing a grinding sound every time she takes a step. She finally makes her way around where Timothy waits.

Timothy stands at the top of the hill gazing down at the farmhouse. He appears to be dazed, almost hypnotized by the armed men looking for him. His shoulders seem rounded and sunken. He doesn't move. He doesn't hide. He merely watches from the vantage point for his destiny to unfold. It's difficult to tell if he was always waiting for them or if he's completely given up on his quest. Perhaps now his mental illness will come to an end. The end is up to him.

With her aching back and stinging arms, Emily creeps up behind Timothy. He begins to turn around just as she swings the butt of the shotgun at his head. The direct blow knocks him down. He kicks around for a moment, but the unconscious darkness prevails. He'll be out for several minutes, just long enough for the police to find him.

Emily flings the shotgun into the dense bushes and runs to her car. The search team is close on her heels. The voices are coming closer to her location. It will only be a matter of moments before the search team discovers her. She turns the key and her rental Jeep ignites. The Jeep takes off down the makeshift dirt road away from an easy exit, but most importantly away from the police.

Emily's heart is pounding in her ears and she realizes that she is breathing too fast. She doesn't even breathe this hard when working out in the gym. Her gut tightens and her vision seems to be impaired. The harder she tries to focus on the road, the dizzier she becomes. Now she's one step away from a full-blown panic attack. There's no time to relax and recover, she punches the gas pedal and speeds on.

The Jeep bounces down the narrow road like a metal bucking bronco. The road is barely wide enough for her small vehicle and it seems to be getter narrower. The overgrown bushes and low hanging tree branches scrape the sides and the roof of her car. The branches obscure her view, and she has no idea whether or not this road will lead her away from the farm and back out to the main road.

The overgrown foliage seems to instantly disappear from Emily's view. She slams on the brakes and the Jeep barely stops before a barbwire fence. She is trapped like a rat with nowhere to go. She throws open her car door and gets out. For a moment, she takes several deep breaths to steady her legs and her equilibrium. She can hear voices approaching and now canines accompany the search team. The barking becomes more intense with each yard of road.

Emily decides that she must move the fence to try and squeeze the car through. The old posts are rotted. She grasps one of the posts and begins to jimmy it back and forth. It breaks free. She begins the same technique with the other post and it crumbles away.

The voices and dogs are gaining speed. The old rusted barbwire is on the ground. Emily quickly pulls the wire away from the posts and winds them out of the way. She can now hear the individual voices of the police search team. No doubt that they have found Timothy where she left him.

Emily gets back into the Jeep and carefully drives under the barbwire. At first, the Jeep won't pass under and the front tires seem to be stuck in a hole. Emily closes her eyes and gives the Jeep a little bit of gas. The car jerks and groans, but finally passes over onto the other property.

There is no road, just an open pasture with tall weeds. She drives as fast as she dares through this vast field. She never looks back or to the left to see if the police are gaining on her. With a big bump, Emily manages to hang onto the steering wheel as she makes contact with the main road leading out of town. She looks in her rearview mirror. There are no law enforcement vehicles or sirens in sight.

She holds her breath for several minutes until she's sure that no one is following her. She pulls the Jeep over to the side of the road and stops. She closes her eyes and takes ten deep slow breaths. Only when her pulse was back at an acceptable level did she continue to slowly drive away. She wanted to get back to the safety of her home as soon as possible. Now Emily can savor the wonderful image of Susie as she is being reunited with her parents.

Chapter 31
Friday 2350 Hours

The evening has turned chilly with a heavy fog layer that has covered the sky and obscured the immediate treetops. It's difficult to ascertain if the moon is full or barely a shiny sliver. In the darkness all native creatures are quiet and not even a leaf is moving in the subtle breeze. It seems to be the end of the universe at this very moment, but proves to be a festive evening for death and torture. Soft moans and frantic breathing is the only sound that fills the evening air.

Compulsion

The Accomplice has taken his sadistic turn in violating the fresh new victim. Just before the strike of midnight, the victim takes her last terrified breath. At least for her, the nightmare is now over. She lays motionless on the ground still restrained with heavy duct tape. Her green eyes are now glazed and motionless. Her petite body is contorted. Her soul has moved on and she no longer feels the pain and anguish of the brutal events. The Accomplice now has great power in his body, mind, and soul to last until the next sacrifice. He feels a tremendous relief and it is time for relaxation.

The Killer now takes his turn of a fierce attack. He must finalize his transition to the ultimate destiny of freedom. He must complete his attack as the bewitching hour proceeds. The violence consumes him. He becomes the Peregrine Falcon in every sense of the hunt and kill process. His teeth tear at the flesh of the neck and shoulders. The excitement of the fresh kill electrifies every cell in his body. The blood is still warm. It is inviting. The tingle throughout his hands and feet encapsulates the beautiful moment. His fantasy of this precise moment comes to life. He has waited so long. So long trolling for the right victim. Executing the right capture. And now the finalization of the kill is almost too much to endure. The Killer looks into the future and sees the freedom of the cosmic energy of mankind. Now it can be all his – the eventual immortality.

It is time now to share one body with another.

The feeling of relief is now upon the Killer and Accomplice. The ritual of merging the last victim to this one begins. They amputate the young woman's right arm and leave the previous victim's arm in its place. The crime scene is almost set. A few more signature touches are applied to the victim's last stand. The Killer and Accomplice are both connected with all of their victims now and forever.

Chapter 32
Saturday 1000 Hours

A fter staying at a motel last night, Emily climbs her stairs to the living room area surrounded by glass and a view of the trees. She drops down on the couch and puts her feet up. She tries to relax after her trip back this morning. Her whole body still aches even after a long hot shower this morning. It feels like she has new bruises on top of old bruises. The doorbell interrupts her poor, pitiful me thoughts. She looks out the deck window and sees Theresa and Sergeant waiting intently.

"Coming", Emily yells. She moves across the living room in moderate pain and descends the stairs, opening the front door with a smile, "Hello."

Sergeant bounds inside and jumps up to greet Emily properly.

"We didn't expect you back so soon." Theresa states.

"It turned out that I didn't need to take a trip; I found what I needed on the Internet." Emily hated lying to her friend. "Come on up, I have some coffee made."

Theresa walks inside and closes the front door. She hands Emily the local morning newspaper, "This was on your porch."

"Thanks." Emily takes the newspaper and leads Theresa upstairs.

Sergeant jumps up the stairs ahead of the women skipping every other step. Emily and Theresa head to the kitchen where there is a fresh pot of steaming coffee. The aroma hits the senses before it can be captured in a mug.

Theresa asks, "You okay dear?"

"Fine." Emily gives Theresa a cup of coffee.

"It's just that you look so tired."

"I've been working on too many assignments at once, that's all."

Theresa points to the newspaper on the counter, "What do you think about the serial killer?"

"What?"

"The serial killer that's on the loose in Santa Cruz. It's right on the front page." She takes a sip of coffee, "I think it's two or three victims. That qualifies as a serial crime doesn't it?"

"I think so." Emily picks up the paper and briefly scans the story. She couldn't believe that there's a serial killer right in her hometown. It's not like it can't happen anywhere, but it unnerves Emily.

"I don't worry about you here alone with Sergeant to protect you." Theresa smiles. Sergeant perks up his ears when he hears his name.

Emily smiles, "That's for sure. Everyone should have a trusty four-legged companion."

Theresa continues, "Oh that nice detective came by to see us yesterday."

"Detective?"

"You know the one that you reported Donald to?"

"Oh yes, of course." Emily remembers how awkward he was trying to apologize to her for his rude behavior. It was cute.

"He's trying very hard to get Donald evicted and out of our neighborhood." Theresa watches Emily with interest. "You think he's handsome don't you?"

"What?"

Laughing, Theresa says, "C'mon Emily, he's a hunk."

"I can't believe you just said hunk."

"Well he is and he asked about you too."

"About what?"

"He just wanted to know where you were. I

guess he came over here first before he came over to talk to me."

"Oh."

Theresa is completely amused by Emily's obvious reaction to the detective, but decides not to tease her anymore.

* * * * *

Emily sits down at her office workstation computer after Theresa leaves and scans local articles as well as national articles referencing the serial killer in her town. It really makes her angry that there is a serial killer in her town. Maybe it's because it hits too close to home or maybe it's because it changes her focus from the child predators.

She then realizes that the homicide photos that she saw on Detective Lopez's desk were probably the serial homicide cases. Her mind wanders back to the detective. She wonders why he's so interested in her wacko neighbor. After all he's a homicide detective, not a community service officer.

The computer cursor is blinking on a blank screen. Emily snaps back to her fact-finding task and begins gathering all of the information about the serial homicide victims. She begins slowly to use her expertise to track down the local serial killer. She does a basic victimology to find the names, ages, and backgrounds of the two women. The news media didn't give much detail about the description of the bodies and crime scene except that they were strangled and dumped.

Emily theorized that there was most likely a definite signature used by the killer and that the women were also sexually assaulted. There must be a fantasy that the killer acts out to feed his compulsive need. She feels extremely revitalized that she has another case to track; and, it's a perk that it's right here in her hometown. Emily feels the driving force inside her, but she must be careful not to make any mistakes and let her guard down; otherwise, her identity will be exposed right in her own backyard.

Chapter 33
Saturday 1100 Hours

P ajaro is a small suburban town in the southern part of Santa Cruz County of barely five thousand, mostly Spanish-speaking residents, which is located in the middle of a huge agriculture region. Much of California's vegetables are grown in the surrounding areas around Pajaro. The famous California artichokes are grown only a few miles away from the crime scene location.

Rick cruises north on Highway 1 exiting at Riverside Drive in Watsonville. He turns down his police radio to give himself some desired peace, even if it's only for a few minutes as he cruises into Pajaro. His thoughts are frenzied and anxious. There have been too many murders in such a short period of time. The serial killer is like a killing machine set to warp drive. There seems to be evidence to support the acts of two serial killers. He contemplates two scenarios of a murder competition in action or just two individuals with the same thirst for blood.

Rick drives past a gas station and a small town market. Another quarter of a mile he spots the familiar emergency vehicles and police cars lined up at attention. The area of interest is large and flat with subtle surrounding hills. He pulls up next to one of crime scene detective's vehicle and parks.

The detective is extremely tired and feels like his entire world is crumbling beneath his feet. Nothing seems to be working out the way it should. He sits in his car for a moment willing more strength and stamina to be able to run this investigation efficiently.

A small roadway just off the main thoroughfare runs right into an old train station. The old Union Pacific train with individual cars still runs through the state carrying lumber, hay, and miscellaneous building materials. It's amazing how there is still a need for railroad engineers in an ever-changing high-tech world.

Rick treks down the short road and observes the taped off crime scene. It makes him uneasy. Compared to the previous crime scenes, this one is out in the open. It's almost like a carefully orchestrated play with a dead body posed to throw the police off the killer's trail. Something doesn't seem right to the detective, but he can't seem to pinpoint the reason. His main hope is that there will be more forensic evidence to connect to the suspects and to the murders.

Rick studies the entire area and locates two old building structures just east on the property that had been used as storage or housed chickens. It's interesting that the body wasn't dumped inside one of those structures, so it's obvious that the killers put this particular victim on display for effect. "But why?" He continues to ponder. He then sees Matt exiting one of the buildings complaining about the stench inside. Ken joins his crime scene partner carrying an evidence bag.

Matt still dramatically coughs and chokes, "That is just nasty. There are all kinds of decomposing smells in there from garbage to rodents."

"Somebody probably had pit bulls housed in there at one time." Ken supposed.

"I wouldn't put my pit bulls in there. It's disgusting."

Ken agrees, "They wouldn't be caught dead in there either."

Matt explains, "You know a pit bull can take down a two hundred pound man in less than two seconds?"

Rick interrupts, "What have you got so far?"

Still grimacing, Ken answers, "We've got Deputy Monahan taking the crime scene photos." He gestures at the body where the deputy seems to be a natural at capturing the different angles for investigative purposes. "We've also got a pretty good set of tire marks once we get a suspect's vehicle to compare to."

Rick asks, "What about the victim's clothing?"

"Nothing so far." Ken continues, "I've got some cigarette butts and a can of soda that don't look very old."

"You never know. Continue to fan out and take note and collect anything that doesn't look like it should be there."

Both Matt and Ken make an exaggerated salute at the detective and go back to their duties of searching the crime scene for potential evidence. Rick tries not to show how annoyed he is with the crime scene detectives.

From studying the crime scene, Rick regards that the body is going to be the most promising for holding any potential evidence. He makes some notes and sketches, and then moves toward the body. The posed body of the young woman is tremendously unsettling.

The victim has been stripped nude and still has the duct tape restraining her one hand and feet. There is additional duct tape that has been placed all the way around her head over her mouth. Her eyes are open and still seem to hold a trace of terror. Her neck has three deep bruise marks showing that she has been strangled more than once. You can't help but be immediately shaken by her frozen pose. She is on her back with her one hand taped to another arm appendage in a strange praying position.

Rick reflects on how the body shows the work of two serial killer offenders from two different organizational techniques. "What is the religious significance and the tearing of flesh", wonders the detective. The obvious macabre signature is the amputated arm from another victim; no doubt that it's the previous victim from the ranch. He tries to piece together if the signature is shared or based on one of the individuals.

The detective knows that the serial killers won't ever stop until he stops them. The burning question is when will he get a break. He considers which will break first, him or the case.

Chapter 34
Sunday 1300 Hours

E mily drives up to the second serial crime scene
location off Larkin Valley Road and parks just
out of immediate view. She gets out of her Jeep
with Sergeant tailing her. The murder scene still has
some crime scene tape fluttering in the breeze. Sergeant sniffs at the broken barbwire fence and raises
a big paw.

"What's up Sarge?"

The dog pads easily through the fence to the location of where the body was found and sniffs

around. Emily follows the dog and studies the location. Several crows fly overhead as the subtle breeze increases. Her immediate question was, "Why did the killer pick this particular location?" It unquestionably adds a dramatic element to the crime, but there must be something more driving him. She wishes that she paid more attention to the photographs she viewed on Detective Lopez's desk.

Emily was able gather a significant amount of information about the women and their backgrounds. She also recruited her good friend Sergeant Sullivan to find out anything from police databases about the investigation. He was able to unofficially get some information about the suspected serial killer. Emily didn't ask him how he got the information, but he said that there were too many elements of the murders to suggest that there was only one killer; most likely there are two killers. That was an intriguing thought to Emily and definitely going to be a considerable challenge for Detective Lopez. She thinks about him for a few minutes before leaving the crime scene.

Emily stops and closes her eyes. She wills the scene to come alive in her mind by imagining what the killers did and didn't do to their victim. In her mind, the dark crime scene seems to give more excitement to the killers without the intrusion of headlights. She sees them working slowly and taking turns, but she can't quite figure out all of their motivations.

Emily opens her eyes again to the present. "C'mon Sergeant, let's go." Sergeant hesitates with all of the wonderful smells tempting him to stay and linger. Emily entices the dog, "Let's go to the beach."

Sergeant happily follows Emily to the car and jumps in riding shotgun. Of course, Emily had other incentives to go to the beach. She wants to see the crime scene area of the first victim at the beach location.

Before hitting the beach, Emily drives by local bars and restaurants trying to pinpoint the locations of where the murdered women were last seen. According to detectives, the women were not seen with anyone they didn't know at these establishments. Emily feels that the women had been under surveillance and followed to somewhat remote locations where they could be abducted or lured into the killer's car.

Emily pulls into the parking lot of Manresa Bar and Pool Hall. She sees Leo, her personal trainer, going into the bar. She's not surprised; many locals frequent the bar for beer and pool. Without stopping, she decides to go down to the beach instead.

Sergeant whines in the passenger seat and presses his nose out of the cracked passenger window.

Emily explains, "We're almost there."

Emily decides to park the Jeep in the little neighborhood of Seascape and walk down the beach trail. She had discovered from reports that the end of the trail was where the body was found. Emily grabs a Frisbee from the back seat and heads down the path with Sergeant trotting obediently at her side. The dog seems to have a sixth sense that he needs to be close to Emily's side. It was more likely that he sensed that something really bad happened on this trail.

The trail walk didn't invoke anything unusual, but there seemed to be the same expression of drama to the location of this crime scene. Emily still tries to connect the crime scenes together. She asks herself what was so significant about these locations. There's another crime scene in Pajaro that she will investigate tomorrow. For now, as the cool off-shore breeze enlivens her senses, she decides to take a few minutes to relax and maybe something in her mind will click.

She kicks off her tennis shoes and peels off her sweatshirt, now dressed in sweats and a tank top. With a big wrist flick action, the Frisbee sails out toward the water. Sergeant gallops into the surf to retrieve his prize. The beach is fairly deserted, only a few joggers and kids playing in the sand. She watches Sergeant jump around in the water, taking extra time before returning to Emily. The sea air is cool and brisk while there's a slight cloud cover blocking some of the sun's rays.

Emily sits down and curls her toes in the sand trying to relieve her mind of ghastly images of death. She manages to locate all of the distinct shades of the sand granules at her feet. A voice stops her intense search and she looks up.

"Hi." Detective Lopez stands in front of her breathing hard from a vigorous run, barefooted and wearing running shorts. His dark t-shirt is soaked with perspiration.

Surprised, Emily replies, "Hi." She tries not to stare at him too closely or admire his muscles.

Sergeant runs up and jumps on the detective with wet sandy paws leaving distinct prints on the front of his shirt.

"Sergeant!" Emily stands up. "I'm so sorry."

Laughing, Rick says, "No big deal. We are at the beach." He gestures around him.

Emily smiles, "I guess you're right." She throws the Frisbee again and watches Sergeant bound into the water. She continues, "So the department actually gave you a day off?"

"Not really the day, but I'm taking a short break to get my thoughts together."

"Oh." Emily pauses for a moment. "Figuring out a way to get rid of my neighbor?"

"Still working on it. Has he been bothering you?"

"No. It's just a little unnerving that he lives only a few feet away." She sits down and watches the hypnotic waves lap at the sand.

Rick sits down next to her and watches the waves too. Sergeant bounds back and lies down with his tongue hanging out looking at Emily and then back to the detective.

Emily takes a long moment before she asks a

question. "Are you making any progress on the serial killer case?"

Rick stares at her for a long moment before answering. "Some." He gets a feeling that she knows more than she's saying. "I could always use some insight."

"Insight?"

"You know your thoughts, opinions, references, maybe you know an eye witness to the crimes."

Emily laughs. "Detective if I didn't know better I'd think you're flirting with me or the very least making fun of me."

He looks at the water with two seagulls swooping overhead, "I would never make fun of you." For the first time in months, he really feels at ease sitting with Emily, even if they don't say a word to one another.

Emily gets up and shakes off excess sand. She's a little embarrassed that the detective made a roundabout compliment to her. "It's nice to see you again detective, but we've got to go."

Standing up and facing her, Rick requests, "Please, call me Rick."

She smiles, "Nice to meet you Rick."

They face each other for an awkward moment. Sergeant jumps around them excited that he has someone else to impress.

The detective offers, "Call me if there's any change with your neighbor. And if you really feel like you're safety is at risk call 911." He studies her face trying to read her, but it's difficult. Her intense dark eyes haunt him, and he notices that her cuts on her face are healing up nicely.

"You'll be the first to know."

"I'm staying at The Beach Inn for a while, so you can reach me there if I'm not at the office numbers."

"Thanks. C'mon Sergeant." Emily smiles and begins to walk back up the trail leaving the detective behind to finish his run.

Emily walks up the trail with a wet happy dog. She can feel the detective watching her go and she dares not to turn around. Part of her enjoys the attention, but part of her is worried that he might get too curious about her.

Rick shifts his weight and slightly stretches his calves as he watches Emily begin to hike up the beach trail. There is more about her than meets the eye. There's something so familiar about her that it actually troubles him. It's not like he knows her from somewhere, but rather like he knows how she thinks.

Chapter 35
Monday 0830 Hours

Police officers and the administrative staff filter into the Sheriff's Office on another hectic Monday morning. For most, coffee seems to be the most important component of the day. Phones are ringing and a few citizens trickle in to pay outstanding tickets, get copies of incident reports, and be fingerprinted for job applications and licenses.

Rick is nursing his third or fourth cup of coffee as he begins to go over phone messages and his plan for follow up investigative interviews. His phone extension rings.

Picking up the receiver, "Lopez Homicide." He listens and then smiles, "Hey Rivas, how's it going?"

Detective Ray Rivas from the Yuma County Sheriff's Office is an old friend of Rick's. They worked together for a short period of time before Rivas moved to Yuma. They managed to stay in touch and even worked a cross-jurisdictional missing person case together.

Detective Rivas says, "Pretty good, not enough hours in the day."

"No kidding, I've got my hands full here."

"I heard about your serial case. Tough break."

"You're not calling about new information on my cases are you?" He said jokingly.

Detective Rivas becomes serious, "No, sorry. But I wanted to ask if there has been any information sent to you about the case."

Detective Lopez frowns, "What do you mean sent to me?"

"Has information been sent to you by email anonymously?"

"No, why?"

"The child serial murder case that I recently closed was because someone sent me information anonymously by email. Of course, it was legit and authenticated, but we never had a clue who sent it or where it came from. It was top investigative stuff, I mean truly exceptional."

"And you think someone would send me information about my serial case?"

Detective Rivas explains, "About a week ago a woman was the victim of a hit and run driver here. She was very lucky to have survived the wreck; her car was totaled, and she had some major computer equipment and surveillance stuff smashed to pieces."

Detective Lopez tunes out the morning chatter around him and listens intently as his stomach begins to tighten.

Detective Rivas continues, "She was released the next day from the hospital. In the meantime, I kept one of her hard drives from her laptop computer that was salvaged from her Explorer. I was actually going to call her to ask if she wants it back, or if we can junk it."

"Don't tell me, your curiosity got the better of you?" Rick has an unsettling feeling in the pit of his stomach.

"Actually, I went to speak with her in the hospital, and my gut was telling me something different than what her answers were telling me. She had several weapons and high-tech computer equipment. And get this, she even had a Beretta strapped to her ankle when she was brought to the emergency room."

Rick listens intently and he has a feeling he knows exactly what his friend is going to say.

"I had forensic services take a look at her hard drive to see if it's just, you know, the usual stuff."

"What did you find?" Detective Lopez could

barely speak.

"The information emailed to me about the child serial killer case originated from that specific hard drive."

"Are you sure?"

"Absolutely, no doubts whatsoever."

"So why are you calling me?" Detective Lopez holds his breath.

"Because this woman lives in your jurisdiction and I thought you might want to look into her background. Maybe she might have information about your killer or about how she gathers information at the very least."

Rick took a deep breath and asks barely above a whisper, "What's her name?"

"Emily Stone."

Chapter 36
Monday 1200 Hours

A dark green Honda is parked a few houses down from Emily's house. Staring straight ahead, the Accomplice sits behind the wheel obscured behind tinted windows. The point of interest is Emily's house; the occupant waits and watches, while the entire time never averting his gaze.

A young neighborhood woman pushing a baby stroller walks by not paying any attention to the parked car or the occupant. A few cars pass by going to their prospective homes or out for the day.

Compulsion

The neighborhood continues to go about the day never knowing that evil was as close as their front yard.

The Accomplice fights to keep his mind in the present. His thoughts wander back to the previous evenings wondrous discovery of death. He can't stay focused in the present without wishing for the sadistic and exciting rerun to continue in his mind. His hands begin to sweat and slightly tremble with anticipation. He grips the steering wheel a little tighter and rotates his wrists.

The front door opens and Emily exits the house carrying a laptop computer and digital camera bag. Her big dog watches her leave from the large picture window upstairs, steaming up the window with his breath. Emily gets into her Jeep and backs out of the driveway, never noticing the man watching her closely and how difficult it is for him to not walk up to her and snap her neck.

Emily drives off down the street. The green Honda slowly pulls away from the curb and follows her.

Chapter 37
Monday 1300 Hours

E mily has been to Pajaro only a couple of times in the past, usually when she was using it as a short cut to get to one of the other surrounding cities. She is amazed by all of the agricultural fields bursting with many varieties of lettuce, broccoli, artichokes, and strawberries. She drives around to a few areas unsure where the crime scene was precisely located. No one pays her any attention and doesn't seem to care that she searches for her investigative location of interest.

Compulsion

Emily slowly drives to the old railroad station down a narrow dirt driveway that opens into a field area with a couple of crumbling buildings. Once again, she is taken by the type of location that the killers use to dump a body. All of the locations where the bodies were discovered were planned for a specific reason that drives the serial criminal's mind. Exactly what drives them is not known yet.

The overgrown-weeded area looked to be an old abandoned farm with a couple of decaying chicken coops and two dilapidated buildings. Emily feels that there must be some religious significance to the crime scene locations for the killers; not religious in the literal term of the word, but a significant psychological fury of the killing experience in order to bring it to a whole new level.

Emily parks the Jeep about twenty feet from one of the structures and gets out to look around. She views the area where the body was found by the trampling of many police issue boots and remnant pieces of police tape. The body appeared to be out in the open, much more visible than the other two locations. To the east side of the property are extremely tall weeds with old neglected shrubs allowing for some coverage or possible escape routes.

The buildings seem to pique Emily's interest the most. She carefully approaches the bigger building that has old plywood nailed over where the windows were once located. Gang tagging in the local colors shows artistic marks on any of the available surfaces to view. There's an unmistakable stench that assaults Emily's senses of something dead, probably rats or maybe something larger like a cat.

Emily feels somewhat vulnerable without her Beretta in an ankle holster for easy accessibility, but she will be fine only poking around the crime scene area. It's not like it's at night in a poverty stricken area. She looks around and listens intently for any close sounds or approaching voices. There's nothing, not even a bird chirping. The wind is still as well, but the sun beats down drying the weeds to a more brittle existence.

Emily finds the door to the structure open a couple of feet. It looks like the detectives have already searched the building during their investigation, but Emily wants to take a look herself. It has been pried open just wide enough for a person to squeeze inside. There is another window on the other side of the building where the plywood is half missing and lying on the ground. At least there will be some air and a little bit of light from the outside.

Emily pushes the door open with her boot and then goes inside to have a look. There's some light coming from the cracks around the decaying structure. It looks like the building was used as a sewer rather than storage. The stench was horrific from unknown liquids by each corner. Emily puts her right hand to her nose and mouth, but still moves deeper inside. Something shiny catches her attention on the floor through another doorway. An old pine door leans up against the wall covered with thick cobwebs. She moves through the second opening

hoping not to attract spiders or any scurrying var-
mints.

Upon closer inspection, the shiny object in question is a key charm of a skull and crossbones. Not
something that is terribly unique. A teenager
could've dropped it, but Emily feels that this was
left by one of the killers to express his need to poison society with his disease. Or rid society of specific types of victims, like that of a poison used to
kill rodents. She picks up the charm and tucks it in
her jean pocket.

Emily is interrupted by a slam against the side
of the building causing her to jump and gooseflesh
to rise on her arms. She turns in the direction of the
noise, but before she can see what's going on the interior completely goes pitch black. The sound of
hammering cuts through the darkness, someone was
nailing the open window shut. She thought she
could hear two soft voices coming from outside.
Someone wanted her confined and unable to escape.
She didn't want to just wait and see what they were
going to do next. No one could hear her if she
screamed, but she knew that was the least of her
problems. She backs up against the cool wall to gain
her bearings and equilibrium in the darkness. She
could feel a slight vibration of her unknown assail-
ants making sure that the window was secure with
no possibility of escape. The unknown muffled
voices seem to banter back and forth with instructions.

There was a low growl coming from the main

room. It started out low and then gradually increased in intensity. There was no mistaking that growl; it was coming from a fierce fighting dog. Emily leans forward in the direction of the doorway and could see a reflection of two canine eyes approaching. She was trapped. If she didn't get out, she was going to be mauled to death by the dog. There would be another murder at the same crime scene, she thought dryly.

The two voices from outside seem to disappear as quickly as they had started. She thought she heard a car drive away. Her mind reels trying to figure out who would want her dead. No doubt it was same two people who broke into her house in the middle of the night. She reprimands herself harshly for not watching for anyone that might be following her.

The pitch-blackness seemed to brighten slightly with each passing moment as her eyes become somewhat accustomed to the shadows. Emily moves slowly with her back against the wall towards the door opening. She knows that the dog will have some trouble tracking her scent through all of the decaying odors. She is about at the doorway opening when the vicious dog tracks her every move and can smell her terror. It's only a matter of seconds before the dog makes contact; Emily won't stand a fighting chance against the powerful jaw and snarling teeth. Her hands are shaking and she can feel her heart pounding in her chest with every breath.

She reaches her hand slowly around the frame of the doorway and grasps the old unhinged door. It's now or never she thinks. Emily grabs the door and braces it in front of her blocking the doorway. The dog pounces toward her with a ghastly growl looking for blood. She holds the doorway strong stopping the dog from entering the room. The dog takes several steps back and then tries to knock the door in toward Emily. Half of the door seems to become wedged in the crumbling doorframe taking some of the weight off of Emily.

Emily spots one of the windows in the room that seems to have daylight shining through the cracks. It may be her imagination, but the cracks seem to be getting bigger. The dog slams against the door again with its muscular body. With every hit, the old boarded up window moves slightly. Emily estimates that she has thirty seconds after she moves from the braced door before the dog breaks through to her. She didn't remember anything lying around in the room that she could use for a weapon or tool. She'll have to hope that the window will give way with her bare hands. The dog slams again against the door with a splintering crash.

Taking a deep breath and willing every ounce of energy throughout her body, Emily takes two steps to the window. She kicks hard with a stomp kick twice and the plywood breaks free. She uses her fists to push out the plywood. Daylight pours inside the filthy room. As she begins to climb out the window, she hears the door splinter and bang for the last time. The dog is close on her heels. She jumps out the window, hitting the ground running. She manages to get her hand on her Jeep door handle and looks back at the building. A black and white pit bull effortlessly jumps through the window, clearing the frame, now coming for blood.

Emily is safely inside her Jeep, but the pit bull continues its pursuit of her. She manages to get the key in the ignition and turn the car on. Slamming the gearshift into drive, she stomps the accelerator and cranks the wheel to the right just as the dog hits her windshield showing its impressive jaw and teeth. She slams on the brakes causing the dog to roll off her hood. Without a second to lose, she floors the gas pedal to the floor and speeds out to the main street of Pajaro. She doesn't stop and pulls right out into traffic with only a one honk from an old pick up truck. She continues at an increased speed, looks into her rearview mirror, but there's no dog in sight.

Chapter 38
Monday 2200 Hours

The tension builds in every pore and in every cell of the Killer's body. It no longer tingles in anticipation for a kill, but rather aches for human destruction. The last kill didn't satisfy him as the previous ones did. It's becoming more difficult to keep focus on the importance of the ultimate freedom rather than the annihilation of anyone that gets in his path.

The Killer drives alone without the assistance of the Accomplice who generally helps to balance his demonic psyche. The Killer frequents the standard trolling grounds for victims from restaurants and bars. This time he's sloppy and doesn't spend the time to investigate the perfect victim and the most opportune time to attack. Now he doesn't care, the compulsive need to satisfy the endless fantasy in his head takes priority over everything else. It's because the killer's way of life is a specific pattern of violence, but it's now sped up to feed the uncontrollable need of murder and mayhem.

The Killer's relentless need for another victim takes him to the Seacliff Bar less than an hour before midnight. A couple of women get into a small sports utility vehicle and drive out of the parking lot. Two potential victims are now out of his grasp. He sees a petite redheaded woman standing by the bus stop waiting for someone or maybe even a customer; it was difficult to decide.

The Killer pulls his truck beside the woman and she seems pleased to see him.

The woman says, "Hi sugar, you lookin to give me a ride?"

The Killer stares at her and responds in a controlled monotone. "Get in."

The woman hesitates and takes a step back away from the truck. It was something in the Killer's eyes that she sensed wasn't right. Even though she had a few drinks, she could sense danger and the man's eyes pierced through her like she wasn't human.

"No thanks, I forgot that I'm suppose to meet a friend." Her voice waivers a bit in her response.

The Killer maintains his anger. "Get in." He repeats.

"No, I don't think so." The woman is now scared and looks across the street.

A couple walks out the front door of the bar chatting about where they are going next. The woman yells to them. "Hey!" The woman runs across the street to the couple and explains to them about the man in the truck.

The Killer is brimming with rage and has no other choice but to speed away. He beats his fists on the steering wheel. The frustration of wrestling with his neurotic morality devours him. He could begin to feel himself slipping into the abyss of uncertainty. He missed an opportunity to gain another step toward his ultimate freedom, but instead the Killer's violent unraveling has now begun and there's no turning back.

Chapter 39
Tuesday 1900 Hours

E mily had almost an entire day to think about who would have trapped her inside that despicable building with a fighting pit bull. Who would want her dead and why? No one knows her true identity. And who would see her as a threat besides a killer she's hunting?

Emily knew what she had to do and she didn't really like it, but she basically had no other choice in the matter. She takes out her medium sized backpack from her closet and begins to fill it with a portable computer CD drive, several CDs, small Canon digital camera, cell phone, two extra pairs of latex gloves, heavy duty plastic coated twine, and two electronic dog collars with remote. She carefully wipes her fingerprints from all of the items before zipping up the backpack.

She glances out the front window and then gazes outside for a moment before going to her bedroom. She changes from her jeans to black stretch exercise pants and a black long sleeved t-shirt. In her lower dresser drawer, she finds a ski cap that can be pulled down over her face. She shuts the drawer and pauses. There's nothing that she can do now about her situation, even if she goes to the police. Her mind wanders to Detective Lopez, her gut tells her that she can trust him, and he would probably be her only true ally. She had to try her plan first and obtain viable evidence and then she would confide in the detective. Maybe then everything would begin to fall into place.

She takes a packed overnight bag, two bankers boxes filled with files, and a portable computer from her closet. From the top shelf of her closet, she takes two Glock 17s and several loaded magazines. Zipped up in a heavy coat is a small zippered wallet with several thousand dollars in cash. She stashes the wallet in her packed overnight bag. Everything seems to be ready and in place. She looks over to Sergeant who has been watching her closely. He knows that she's planning on leaving him again.

Emily takes a couple of deep breaths to summon

all of her available energy and courage before she leaves her house. Her pulse rate is heightened, but not erratic and unstable. She looks out the window again and notices that her neighbor's truck is gone. She decides to gamble that he won't be back for at least an hour. That should give her enough time.

She packs her Jeep with her belongings, boxes and weapons. Everything is packed except her backpack, which she now slings on her back. She goes through her garage where there is a door that opens on her neighbor's side and other nosey neighbors will most likely not see her enter the premises.

Emily moves to the neighbor's house and spies a downstairs window that's conveniently open. She knows that he doesn't have any dogs, but she's careful not to trip any booby traps or alarms. This man is bizarre and may have some type of security system in place. She puts on a pair of latex gloves and easily opens the window wide enough for her to get through and pulls herself up and through the window without incident.

Standing alert, Emily looks around carefully before she puts one foot forward. The house is cluttered with junk and thrift store items, with stacks of boxes of miscellaneous papers everywhere. It's difficult to move through the chaotic mess. There's a distinct smell of mold, dirty clothes and old trash. She exits the storage bedroom and climbs the cluttered stairs to the living room. She finds a computer on a kitchen table humming. With a sudden movement of the mouse, the computer screen lights up with a desktop background of a busty brunette obviously from some porno movie.

Emily clicks on various desktop icons and immediately locates hundreds of porno sites. She tries some of his folders and finds pages of letters to himself about killing women complete with a list of names. Disturbing images appear of bondage and torture. The various files and images repulse Emily as she quickly retrieves her portable disk drive. She quickly plugs the USB port into his computer and begins to copy various files of interest. While the files are copying, she takes out her digital camera and takes photos of the interior of the house, computer, credit card receipts, bank account, address book, and cell phone records. She takes more photos of the strange artwork and cluttered items throughout the house in order to study later. She notices some additional scribbled art of skull and cross bones; it seems to match the keychain she found at the abandoned building.

The copied files are done. Emily takes the time to gather information about his recent downloads and net surfing activities. She copies another CD with this information. She knows that she has little time before he returns.

She quickly returns everything back into her backpack except the twine and dog shock collars. She quickly makes her way to the garage, it was packed full of boxes and it was difficult to move through the mess. It takes her a moment to find the fuse box and she flips all the switches off. There's nothing that she can do now but wait as it begins to get dark.

* * * * *

Donald drives up in his dusty Ford Truck and parks haphazardly in the driveway. He gets out and mumbles phrases under his breath because he didn't get paid enough for the work he did on a ranch in Watsonville. He fumes as he walks up to the front door and inserts his house key in the lock. He turns the key and pushes the door wide open and slams it shut with disgust. He stands for a moment at the entrance threshold, almost waiting for something or remembering something that he might have forgotten.

The house is extremely dark, and he thought that he remembered that he kept the hallway light on. He flips the switch several times but nothing happens. It's still dark. He trudges his overweight body up the stairs to the landing and moves toward a living room lamp. Just as he's about to switch on the lamp, he's ambushed from behind. He's thrown forward and down on the floor with a significant amount of force and a thin rope is slipped over his hands and feet. Before he can respond with any retaliation attempts, the rope is secured tightly on his hands and feet behind his back in a hogtie position.

He's trapped and incapacitated. His deep pent up anger begins to surface, but the more he struggles the tighter his restraints become. Someone turns him over and rolls him up against the wall. He can see a trim black figure wearing a ski mask. The figure takes some type of collar and belts it around his neck and another around his right upper thigh. The figure cinches the neck restraint even tighter. He has a difficult time swallowing and tries to focus intently on who is standing over him. If he could just loosen one of his wrists, he could overpower this intruder. He keeps twisting and turning his wrists as they begin to burn from the friction of the rope restraints. Tiny droplets of blood begin seeping from the wounds.

Emily stands above Donald, now in charge over this neighborhood bully. Her thoughts become jumbled because she wants desperately to make him pay for what he did to her and the nice elderly people on the street. She gets a grip on her emotions and continues with her original plan. There's only a little bit of time before he can wriggle out of the restraints.

"Why did you break into the house next door?" She demands with a strange voice inflection from a voice scrambler that she bought off the Internet some time ago.

"Blow me." He manages to say.

Emily presses the remote button, causing an electric surge to penetrate Donald's neck and thigh. He winces in pain.

"I'm going to ask you one more time. Why did you break into the house next door?"

Donald looks up at Emily almost as if he can see

right through the ski mask. He has a look of recognition. "I know who you are, take that mask off you coward."

Emily presses the button again, this time she holds down the button for a couple of seconds.

She leans into Donald and says, "You've been warned only once." She tosses the remote next to him.

Emily turns and heads down the stairway and out the way she entered. Her pulse is racing and she finds it hard to catch her breath. It's going to be fifteen maybe twenty minutes before Donald is free and he's going to come looking for her. She jumps out the bedroom window and reenters her house.

Chapter 40
Tuesday 2100 Hours

Emily pulls into The Beach Motel's parking lot that's located just a block from the main beach area. She was still feeling guilty about dumping Sergeant on her neighbors at this hour, and she could see their concern about her somewhat erratic behavior. Her adrenaline is still pumping and not showing any signs of slowing after the aggressive episode with her neighbor.

Now she has to get some distance from her work, her life, and the serial murders in her town by going to Valparaiso, Indiana. She has about a thirty-two hour drive ahead of her and plenty of time to think along the way.

As she sits in her car staring straight ahead at the motel, she wrestles with her conscience. Is she doing the right thing? Can she really trust Detective Lopez? She sees an open curtain and can see him seated at a desk with several files open and photographs strewn on the floor and bed. A couple of empty beer bottles sit nearby. She continues to watch him for a few minutes and sees that he's struggling with his own demons as he stares at the photographs. She can't help but feel for his difficult position; she has been there several times before.

It seemed strange that he's staying at this motel, but maybe it's a way for him to get the solace he needs to work the demanding cases. She still continues to watch him as he runs his hands over his face trying to will the answers he so desperately seeks. He looks tired and frustrated.

Emily opens her car door and gets out. She hesitates again before going to his door. She decides to softly knock and wait.

The door opens and Rick blinks in surprise. "Hi."

Emily replies, "Hi."

"You okay?" He says with genuine concern.

Emily is hit hard like a ton of bricks on top of her head just by that simple little question. Her emotions are suddenly unstable and she's not able to respond right away. She looks stressed and doesn't answer him.

Rick softens and senses that it's extremely difficult for her to be there. "Wait right here." He goes to the mini refrigerator and takes out a six-pack of Heinekens and puts them into a paper bag. "C'mon, you look like you could use some fresh air."

Rick leads Emily out of the motel parking lot down a stairway towards the beach with the bag under his arm. They walk down the stairs in silence. Emily has never felt this emotionally distraught ever in her entire life. It's as if everything has finally come crashing down around her, and she's not quite sure how to proceed. Or if she'll ever be able to forge ahead.

Rick stops at a sandy hill just short of the serene shoreline. The beach is dark and deserted, but the three quarter moon illuminates the bay. The cool feeling of the evening is crisp and invigorating.

"C'mon sit down." He takes a seat in the sand and takes a beer out of the bag.

Emily's mind is racing and she is quite unsteady on her feet. She sits down and tries to concentrate on the sparkling water.

Rick pops the caps off of two beers and hands Emily one.

"Thanks." She obliges and takes a sip of the ice-cold beverage. The distinct flavor stings on the way down her throat zapping her back into reality.

Rick watches Emily closely. He notices that her beautiful eyes look haunted and even scared. He has several questions for her, but he's going to take it slow.

He leans back and enjoys his beer. "Now, are you feeling better?"

Emily stares at the water. She knows if she looks at the detective everything will come spilling out.

"I think you have some very heavy things on your mind." He carefully pushes.

"You could say that."

"But you came to see me." He looks at her curiously.

"Yes."

He touches her arm to get her attention. "Tell me what's going on?"

Emily dares to look at the detective. "I just." And that was all it took, she couldn't hold back the tears anymore. She immediately gets to her feet and wants to flee, to just run away from her feelings and everything that she has been struggling with for so many years.

Rick stops her. "Wait a minute."

"Look I made a mistake, I'm sorry that I bothered you."

Without anything to lose, Rick blurts out, "I know you sent information to the Yuma Police Department about the child murders."

Emily stares at the detective unable to move. It was like her feet were cemented deep in the sand.

"Look, it's okay, no one else knows. Just tell me what's going on." He gently takes her hand and leads her back to where they were sitting. "Who are you?"

Emily could barely speak. "What do you mean?"

"Who do you work for?"

"No one."

"You just hunt down serial killers for fun?"

Emily takes a breath and is silent for a few minutes before she begins. She has never told a living soul about her work and it was difficult to put it into words at this precise moment. She begins to explain about how her parents were killed, and how she vowed to do anything that she could to help victims and their families.

Rick was patient as she explained how she would track the killers and her specific type of investigative techniques. Most importantly, she explained why she couldn't let anyone know her identity. Everything just poured out of her; it was as if she was confessing her lifetime of sins. She was actually beginning to feel better. She took several long drinks of her beer to help steady her nerves now that the truth was out in the open – vulnerable for everyone to see.

"Well?" Emily asked.

Rick was taking in everything that Emily had told him. He was amazed and duly impressed by her effective efforts and how she was able to be so successful in her searches. He knew that she was telling him the truth.

Emily continued, "Please say something. I know

it seems more like a Hollywood movie, but I'm telling you the truth."

"I actually don't know what to say." He smiles. "You're amazing. You track down these serial killers by yourself with equipment that you purchase at a computer Internet store or Radio Shack?"

"Pretty much." Emily laughs both in embarrassment and relief.

He really studies Emily and now he has a renewed respect and admiration for her. This beautiful petite woman hunts out serial killers alone. It doesn't get any better than that in the detective's mind.

"Now what?" Emily says with some nervousness.

"Don't worry, no one will ever know what you just told me."

"Ok." Emily stares into the detective's eyes for a few tense moments, but catches herself and looks away. For the first time since she was a child, she feels safe and secure even if it's just for a short time staring at the Monterey Bay.

Trying to change the awkward moment, Emily asks, "How's your case going?"

"Not very well."

"Want a fresh pair of eyes?"

Chapter 41
Tuesday 2300 Hours

The Killer drives alone through the quiet neighborhoods looking for signs of life that will fulfill his own morbid fantasy. Houses are dark, with only a few who have porch lights illuminated to keep prowlers away. The occupants are safely inside fast asleep.

The Killer can't sleep. Every time he closes his eyes he sees through the eyes of the Peregrine Falcon flying high over the shoreline relentlessly searching for his next prey. When awake, he's relentlessly searching for his next prey at bars, restaurants, and shopping centers. It's become a way of life and ultimate survival. He won't sleep again until the next phase has been completed. The only way the Killer can survive in this life and move into the next is by sacrificing another victim. He continues to search mercilessly, but now with a renewed energy that has been instilled in his psyche. He is on a mission of human destruction so he can live ultimately free.

The Killer notices a woman walking alone. Before he can respond, the woman gets into a car with a man. How lucky for her, he thinks. He keeps searching.

Chapter 42
Tuesday 2330 Hours

E mily is seated on the floor of the motel room studying the crime scene photos for each of the murders. She has arranged the photos by importance to the serial killer. She feels a little light-headed after drinking a couple of beers, but extremely relaxed considering everything she has been through.

Rick watches her work and can't believe how naturally things come to her. She is expertly ordering the photos and lists probable suspects and where the suspects and victim's paths could've crossed. He had worked with many detectives and police officers in the past, but none had the natural intuition and tenacity that Emily exhibits.

Emily says, "You do understand that this killer is driven by compulsion and won't stop until you stop him?"

"That's becoming apparent."

"He's not going to just let you arrest him either, he definitely won't go quietly. He'll take collateral damage with him if he can." She holds up a close up photo of the tear marks on one of the victim's neck. "He somehow thinks that he's going to become something else."

"What do you mean by something else?"

She leans back against the bed. "Like he's becoming another person or thing in his mind that will give him the ultimate power. It's power he seeks unlike his partner who seeks another kind of power in the domination and torture over women."

"So the amputation is all a part of him becoming whatever he's fantasized about and not just a trophy?"

"Exactly. In his mind all of his victims are a part of him and in turn they are all a part of each other. That's his supreme power."

"What a pair." The detective leans back in his chair exhausted. "How would these two killers even meet?"

Emily shakes her head, "Who knows, but I'd guess that they have something in common. Maybe they met somewhere recently or some unusual circumstances put them together. Whatever it is they both feel that they have a specific purpose, and they need one another in order to carry out that special purpose." She yawns. "I'm sorry, it's late for me."

Rick looks at his watch and stands up. "It's just past midnight and it's been a long day for me too."

Emily moves the organized photos and profile list toward the desk. She gets to her feet. She faces Rick, but doesn't know exactly what to say. She's already poured her guts out to him and looked at grisly crime scene photos, but now she's at a loss for words. She can't seem to shake his gaze or his unmistakable desirability.

The lamp on the nightstand flickers. It flickers several more times and then the bulb goes out completely. The room is now dimly lit, but Emily and Rick don't move from each other's gaze.

Emily manages to say, "Well I guess that's my cue to go." She turns to leave and walks to the door.

Rick follows her and says, "You sure that you're okay now?"

Emily turns and replies, "I'm okay. Thanks." She smiles.

Ever since the day he saw her on the beach with her dog, he couldn't get her out of his mind. And now, she's confessed her role as serial killer hunter to him, and he's not going to let her go so easily. He feels her attraction to him, but she's guarded, waiting for his response to her. She trusts him, but doesn't want to force the situation. That much the detective knows for sure.

Rick decides to makes his move. He gently takes her left arm and says, "Wait." She turns, but not with a questionable look on her face, it was more of an answer that he wanted.

She looks away for a tense moment and says, "I don't know if."

The detective leans in and kisses her, softly at first. Emily responds with intense heat as they both become embroiled in each other's arms for several minutes, probing each with affectionate kisses.

They move over to the bed and slowly undress each other as their anticipation rises. Emily runs her hands down the detective's chest and then she un-buckles his belt. The detective responds and recip-rocates, he continues to undress Emily.

Rick then begins to make love to her slowly and passionately for several hours. Neither one knew that they possessed that much energy and hunger for one another. Afterward, they both gently fall asleep satisfied and never wanting to be without the other. It was as if there wasn't another soul that could un-derstand what drives each of them.

Emily suddenly awakens. The clock reads a quarter to five in the morning. She sees Rick still sleeping peacefully and doesn't want to disturb him. He desperately needs his rest. She quietly gets dressed and then stands silently next to the bed watching him sleep. It pains her to leave him, now that she's finally found him. They are more con-nected than she even realizes.

Compulsion

Emily knows that she must get away for a while to think and come up with a new strategy; no one is safe with her until these outstanding cases are solved. Someone wants her dead, and she can't take the chance that someone else will get caught in the middle, especially someone she cares deeply about. She must continue with her original plans of leaving town for a while.

She knew if she woke Rick up he would only convince her to stay and that they would work everything out together. She can't compromise his safety. She will return soon. She hesitates for another couple of minutes just to be near him, watching him sleep peacefully before she leaves the motel.

Chapter 43
Wednesday 2130 Hours

The small apartment building was located just four blocks from the beach in Santa Cruz. It was a no frills apartment building for working professionals who don't want the responsibility for the upkeep of front or back yards. The people who live in this apartment building don't have any pets and usually work long or unusual hours. Even at this late hour, many of the occupants aren't home.

The interior of Matt's apartment was basic in décor with only the necessities to live. The furniture is sparse throughout the two-bedroom floor plan and comfortable. Matt sits on the couch with his feet on the oak coffee table complaining to Ken. The television is turned to some reality show rerun with the volume turned down.

"This job is getting so boring. With or without a serial killer on the loose." Matt takes a swig of his domestic beer.

"It's the town." Ken replies casually watching the television set.

"So what you're saying if I want more excitement transfer to a big city?"

"Maybe."

"It'll just be full of ten times more Detective Lopez's out there. One is enough."

"I'm just saying that there's more to do and more opportunity that's all." Ken looks at his partner.

"Maybe you're right." He looks at a beautiful blonde on the television. "Maybe there would be more unsuspecting babes in a bigger city."

"But these cases are driving me nuts. How can you stand Lopez?"

"We have a job to do." Ken opens another beer.

"Doesn't he bug the crap out of you?"

"Not really."

Matt joins his partner and opens another beer. "He's so annoying with his criminal profiles and psychological theories. It doesn't matter how many profiles he writes, the killers are going to be right under his nose anyway."

Ken replies matter of fact, "He's solved more cases than anyone else at the department."

"Big whoop. It still doesn't mean that he's not annoying."

"Maybe not." Ken smiles.

Matt continues to vent, "This town wouldn't know how to catch a killer it they crawled up their ass. Even if the killer walked right into the station and yelled at the top of their lungs, 'I'm your killer'."

"You have good point. Our detective supervisor will never catch the killers." Ken continues to watch the television.

"Touché." Matt taps his beer bottle to Kens.

"Let's go out and do something." Ken says.

"Sure, I'm up for it."

Chapter 44
Thursday 0130 Hours

Emily's neighborhood is quiet. A cat slinks down the side of the street looking for the mouse that belongs to the scent it has been tracking for the past hour. It skirts under a parked car when two men dressed in dark clothing move swiftly around the Brandon's house and disappear into the back yard.

It is quiet inside the Brandon's house; they have been asleep for a couple of hours. Sergeant sleeps on a comfortable doggie bed in the garage so that he won't bother the Brandon's sleep. The dog sleeps deeply dreaming of wide-open meadows and chasing butterflies. His paws gently twitch with each deep breath.

Two masked figures easily open the large sliding door leading into the living room. It barely makes a sound even in the deathly quiet night. They slip inside the house never uttering a word to one another. One of the masked figures gently closes the slider. They both then make their way toward the bedrooms down a long narrow hall without making a single sound. The bedroom at the end of the hall has the door closed.

One of the masked figures gestures to the other to open the closed door. The other figure steadily opens the door with a gloved hand revealing the spacious bedroom. Theresa and Robert are sleeping peacefully and haven't been disturbed by the intruders. The heavy drapes are pulled tight over the windows to keep any unnecessary light from creeping into the room.

The bedroom is located at the back of the house, so it's unlikely that anyone will hear any noise coming from the bedroom. Each intruder stands on opposite sides of the bed and stares down at the sleeping couple for a moment. They each remove a firearm and take aim. With a nod from one of the intruders, Theresa and Robert are violently awakened with the two intruders pressing a gun against their heads. Terrified the couple cries out trying desperately to wake from their nightmare.

Compulsion

In a seething whisper one masked intruder demands, "Where is Emily Stone?"

Theresa responds through sobs, "I don't know."

He repeats again, "Where is she?"

Again, Theresa answers, "I don't know."

Sergeant is barking wildly from the garage and clawing at the closed door.

Robert tries to explain, "We don't know. She came by and said she was leaving and didn't tell us where. She usually doesn't."

The masked intruder strikes Robert leaving a bleeding gash across his forehead. Theresa screams out in terror.

The other masked intruder leans into Theresa and threatens in a quiet voice, "If you're lying we'll be back to kill you."

The two masked men quickly leave the bedroom and disappear out the sliding door. Robert manages to sit up and nurse his deep wound.

Theresa frantically picks up the phone from the nightstand and dials 911.

Chapter 45
Friday 1000 Hours

Emily is still exhausted from the long drive to Indiana since she drove straight through only stopping for gas and food when absolutely necessary. She didn't even have a chance to check her voice mail for messages because she didn't want to talk to Rick right now until she got her bearings and some much needed rest. She was able to get some restful sleep in a motel just outside of town before setting out to find her close friend and confidant Sergeant Mike Sullivan.

Compulsion

The town looks too good to be true and it's hard to imagine that there are still towns in the United States that are clean, relatively free of crime, with friendly inhabitants and neighborly people. Driving through town, Emily realized how much she has missed the scenery as well are her friend Mike.

Emily knows that at ten in the morning he will most likely be at a local favorite establishment called The Steaming Mug for his morning break. She smiles and reflects that he will probably be eating a decadent pastry dripping with chocolate and sugar sprinkles, but will rationalize that he'll start his diet tomorrow.

Emily pulls up in front of The Steaming Mug next to a police patrol car and parks. She quickly gets out and enters the coffee house. Not being disappointed, she spots Mike sitting at a small table reading the newspaper with a half eaten bear claw on his plate.

Emily smiles and says, "I thought you were on a diet."

Mike looks up and gasps, "Em!" He jumps up from the table and gives his friend a bear hug. "It's so good to see you. When did you get here?"

"Late last night and then I came straight here."

"Why didn't you let me know you were coming?" He gestures to sit down at the bistro table.

Taking a seat, Emily continues, "Well I really didn't know until the last minute."

"Where are you staying?"

"I'm not sure yet."

Mike studies his friend carefully and senses her stress. "What's going on Em?"

Emily stares down at the table. It's difficult for her to put into words. "Mike, it's been bad."

Mike is concerned. "Did something happen on one of your investigations?"

"No, well yes and no." Emily becomes frustrated.

"Which is it?"

"I started tracking a serial killer in Santa Cruz and I." She hesitates before continuing, "And I think he's after me now."

"How is that possible?" Mike is very concerned, but pleased that she decided to come home.

"I've been followed and some masked men broke into my house in the middle of the night to threaten me."

"Did you go to the police?"

"Well yes, but for another reason. You know that I can't let them know too much about me." She begins to pick at a corner piece of the bear claw.

Mike leans back and relaxes. "I know, but I'm glad you decided to come out here for awhile. We'll figure this thing out, okay."

"I was hoping that you might have one of your rentals available for a week or so."

"As a matter of fact I do. I'm remodeling one of my duplexes, and you're welcome to stay there for as long as you like." He takes her hand. "Carol and I would love for you to stay with us. I know the kids want to see you too."

Compulsion

"Thank you, but I really need to be alone so I can think this whole situation out."

"I understand, stay as long as you like." Mike knows that there's more to Emily's grief than she's telling him, but he'll give her time – for now.

Chapter 46
Friday 1045 Hours

Donald storms around Emily's house looking for an open window or sliding door. He knew that she must have gone somewhere else so he couldn't confront her about her attack on him. Did she actually expect him to not figure out that it was her? It took him almost forty-five minutes to loosen the rope from his wrists so he could escape. His back was killing him from the assault. He should really think about suing her for assault and ruining his personal property. He knew that she was trouble for him the first time he laid eyes on her. Why didn't the whole neighborhood see his point of view? The rage begins to boil in his blood the more he thinks about Emily and the attack. His heartbeat pounds in his ears making it difficult to concentrate.

Donald observes that the sliding door to the bedroom is barricaded over with heavy cardboard and duct tape. It's the perfect entrance and no one will ever know he's gained access into the house. He quickly pulls the cardboard from the window frame and steps inside Emily's bedroom. He moves through the house and up the stairs not quite sure what to look for. A room off of the dining room proves to be promising.

Donald walks into the small den; it seems to be Emily's office. He begins searching through bills and miscellaneous paperwork on the computer desks. He finds several notes from Valparaiso Indiana from an M. Sullivan. There is a cell phone bill that shows many calls to Indiana – the same phone number. He spends a few more minutes looking through files and the filing cabinet but nothing captures his attention. He writes down Emily's cell number and all the information he could find about M. Sullivan in Indiana. Now at least, he has a place to start to locate her. Emily Stone will wish that she never set foot in his house. He will make sure that she never interferes with his life again.

Chapter 47
Friday 1145 Hours

Rick shuffles through an increasing pile of paperwork on his desk not paying any special attention to details or call back requests. His mind keeps returning to Emily. He hadn't heard from her for two days and she's not answering her cell phone. Her neighbors don't know where she went. Most disturbing is that two men wanting to know Emily's whereabouts attacked them in the middle of the night. It was the same night that Emily came to him searching for support and understanding.

Compulsion

A single thread delicately balances everything, but that thread can break at any moment. That is how the detective feels about everything spiraling out of control in his so-called life. He surmises that Emily is connected to everything in some way, either directly or indirectly. But how, he's not sure about anything. His feelings for her have definitely clouded his judgment to see things objectively. He's never met anyone like her before and probably will never again. It hit him deeply when he awoke to find that she wasn't there beside him. It felt more like a pleasant dream from the night before.

The phone rings at his desk extension and interrupts his nonwork related thoughts. It was a forensic scientist from the San Jose Forensic Laboratory contacting him regarding the last homicide crime scene in Pajaro. It was absolutely unbelievable news, and it couldn't have come at a better time. The lab was able to get a positive nine-point match on a left index fingerprint of the killer from the duct tape, in addition to blood evidence found at the scene that didn't belong to the victim. The semen evidence was too diluted and contaminated for any type of identification. But two out of three certainly isn't bad news.

Rick's blood immediately runs cold and he can barely breathe. The office seems to be shrinking around him and running out of fresh breathable air. Both positive pieces of evidence from the Pajaro crime scene undeniably pointed just to one suspect.

The killer was Donald Everett, Emily's next-door neighbor.

* * * * *

Several police vehicles and two unmarked detective cars are parked in front of Donald's house executing a search and arrest warrant. Breaking into the front door to gain entry to the house, uniformed police officers disperse to verify that it's indeed empty. All is clear.

Rick asks Matt, "Where's Ken?"

"He's taking a personal day." Matt responds.

Rick and Matt begin their search of the house. The crime scene detective begins the search of the downstairs bedrooms by identifying and photographing potential pieces of evidence. Deputy Monahan assists with overall photographs throughout the interior and exterior of the house.

Rick puts an all points bulletin out on Donald Everett with the license plate of his truck and smaller car. He is considered armed and extremely dangerous. It should be cautioned to all law enforcement that when trying to apprehend, the suspect would most likely not be taken in alive.

Matt approaches Rick. "Take a look at this."

The detective follows Matt to the kitchen table where there are many yellow note pads next to the computer. There is a list of people that Donald wants dead with disturbing crude drawings and incoherent doodles next to each name. The pencil that

Donald used was driven so deeply into the paper that several sections of the note pad are imbedded with lead fragments, clearly showing his anger and rage.

Matt continues reading as he flips through several more pages, "I've never seen anything like this before, have you?"

Rick studies the writing. "No, but it clearly fits the behavior pattern left by the killer at the crime scene. Be sure to bag everything."

"You got it." Matt carefully organizes the written evidence before dropping each note pad into specific evidence bags.

Rick continues to survey the house which has an abundant level of pornography portraying the humiliation and brutalizing of women. But interestingly, there are many photos that have been torn out of wildlife and environmental magazines of birds – specifically the falcon. He ponders why this bird is so important to him. The bird is a fierce hunter with incredible speed and agility. He remembers what Emily had said to him about the killer wanting to become something else. It's possible that Donald sees himself becoming the Peregrine Falcon, and that's why he kills. As twisted as that sounds, it seems like the only logical explanation at the moment to the detective.

Rick takes out his cell phone and tries to call Emily's house again – no answer. He tries her cell phone again, but it goes directly to her voice mail. He then notices a small piece of paper on the coffee table with Emily's name on it and how Donald wants to kill her in step-by-step graphic detail. The disturbing images concern Rick even more about Emily's safety.

Before the detective hits the end button on his cell phone, Deputy Monahan approaches him.

"Sir?" Deputy Monahan looks bright-eyed, bursting with important information.

"What's up Monahan?"

"Sir, there's a freezer in the garage." He hesitates, "It's leaking."

Rick follows the deputy to the cluttered garage where one body can barely move around. In one corner there's an old chest freezer with tattered boxes stacked on top. There's a padlock securing the freezer. From one corner drips a sticky dark fluid.

Rick instructs Monahan, "Cut it." He removes several boxes as the deputy uses bolt cutters to easily snap the lock free from the freezer. Matt joins the group to view the freezer contents with various types of evidence bags and containers. With only a slight hesitation, Rick flips the latch up and opens the chest freezer. Sitting directly on top of multiple plastic wrapped contents is a single severed woman's arm. It looked fresh from a week or two. Rick had little doubt that this arm would belong to anyone else except the female victim in Pajaro. It eerily waits to be added to another murder crime scene as it seems to stare back at the police officers.

Rick instructs, "Monahan get several shots of

this." He waits while Deputy Monahan takes several photographs for documentation.

Matt prepares to collect the appendage evidence for transport. He carefully begins to unfold the heavy plastic to reveal a torso, detached head, one severed arm, and severed legs of what appears to be an unidentified dark haired woman. It's unclear if the body parts belong to one person.

"God, I wonder if this is one person or multiple victims?" Matt ponders aloud.

"We won't know until the medical examiner confirms the identity or identities." Rick takes a step back to allow Deputy Monahan to continue with photo documentation.

Rick has a new sense of urgency in this serial murder case. The good news is that they have identified the serial killer, but the bad news is that he's now hunting Emily.

Chapter 48
Friday 1630 Hours

Rick's exhaustion has finally begun to take hold of his body and mind. He hasn't been able to stop and enjoy the fact that the serial murder case has been solved, but rather he dreads the finality of what is yet to come. His limbs feel heavy and fatigued. His eyes are gritty like he has picked up fine sand granules that are trying to flush his tear ducts. No one would fault him for taking a break or a day off. Still, he decides to stop at the Sheriff's Center at the local shopping center.

Compulsion

Rick sits in his car for several minutes getting his thoughts together before going into the office. His mind is on complete overload with all of the information that has been exposed. In actuality, he's the one that feels extremely exposed. It's Friday and the day as well as the week is almost over, but he decides to investigate one more thing that has been plaguing him before he leaves for the day.

He enters the deserted office and sits down at a desk in the back. He plugs in his laptop computer and accesses the criminal justice database. Within a few minutes, he types in the name Emily Stone and her approximate date of birth. He continues to enter all of the pertinent information and waits for a response.

Rick smells old coffee that hasn't been sitting around too long in the office. He decides to brave it and pour himself a cup. The officer that was just here barely had enough time to turn the coffee maker off before responding to a call.

Rick sits down at stares at the computer screen which seems to take an eternity to cough up any information. Several strings of information finally scroll across the screen about Emily. The most interesting information that captured his attention was from Valparaiso, Indiana. Rick realizes that many things make sense about Emily, and he now knows why she seems to have a gift for criminal profiling and crime scenes. Emily Stone was a Deputy Sheriff for the Porter County Sheriff's Office for six years. Then all of her information dropped off the radar for more than four years – until now.

Emily was born and raised in Indiana. Her parents were killed in robbery when she was twelve. She was then sent to live with her uncle here in California and moved back to Indiana after college to become a police officer. It looks as if she moved back here after she resigned and after the death of her uncle. She inherited his moderate estate and home in which she still resides.

Rick is too tired to be entirely surprised by Emily's background. He felt a definite kinship with her and now he knows why, being a fellow cop. It's still a mystery as to why she resigned from the police department and moved out here. There's still just as many unanswered questions as there are answered. Rick digs through her records a little bit more and finds out that her sergeant as well as the person who was listed as an emergency number in her employment records was Sergeant Mike Sullivan.

Chapter 49
Friday 1700 Hours

D onald has been traveling east on California Interstate 680 as the police were searching his house. He was unaware that his fingerprint and blood were found at the Pajaro crime scene, obviously because of his sloppy murdering workmanship. His only priority now is to find Emily and kill her and anyone else who dares to get in his path. This inconvenience of driving to the state of Indiana is all her fault. Her meddling and indignation will soon be her downfall as she gasps her last breaths of this life. He should have killed her that night while she was sleeping. The thought of her suffering has heightened his energy level, which had been dwindling fast over the past few days. His Accomplice rides silently next to him feeling his intense killing energy.

The traffic is heavy and slow moving as he reaches Sacramento during the after work commuting hours. Donald decides to pull off to get something to eat. Both Killers have an almost insatiable appetite, which hardly ever goes completely away. There is a restaurant with few cars in the parking lot that looked like a good place to spend an hour. The small out of the way diner serves up greasy hamburgers with all of the fixings, and pork chops were the special of the day. The men had hamburgers piled high with the works, French fries, onion rings, and several Cokes. They stuffed their bodies to help suppress their compulsion to kill. They must save up their energies to torture and kill Emily in the appropriate amount of time. They ate in silence.

When Donald and the Accomplice were done with their dinner, they exited out the back door to the parking lot. The sound of bottles breaking on the pavement rattles the calm silence. The Killers stop for a moment, look at one another, and then decide to investigate. At the far end of the parking lot sit two junked out abandoned vehicles. The windows have been smashed out and some red and black gang graffiti marks one of the passenger's doors with distinct territories. Two rusted dumpsters with

an abundance of juvenile tagging are tucked in behind the cars. A scraggly, gray-haired homeless
man searches through the dumpsters looking for
bottles and cans. He has two large garbage bags
filled halfway with his recovered, recycled loot.

The homeless man mumbles something to himself as he continues with his tedious quest. He
didn't even have a chance to look up to see the large
hunting knife expertly pierce his heart. The Accomplice retracts the knife with the efficiency of a sushi
chef. The homeless man drops to the ground with a
profound look on his face, an almost peaceful expression. Blood begins to seep from the dying
man's mouth. Donald and the Accomplice stand
over him and watch him slowly die, his life recedes
slowly away as he takes his last two breaths.

Donald feels a new sense of positive energy as
he helps the Accomplice heave the dead man into
one of the dumpsters and slams the lid. This trip
might not be so bad, he thought. There are some
definite perks to satisfy him along the way. It will
be good therapy for him to relieve some of his boil-
ing energy by killing some interesting victims in
various towns.

The Killers get into the car and proceed to leave
Sacramento. Donald continues his journey of discovery and takes the California Interstate 80 heading east. The Killers are coming.

Chapter 50
Saturday 0900 Hours

Rick was lucky enough to get a flight departing at nine last night from San Jose to Chicago. He would have to drive the rest of the way if he was going to meet Sergeant Mike Sullivan in person. He had no doubts that Emily was staying nearby and hopefully the sergeant would accommodate his request to find out her precise whereabouts.

It takes approximately an hour to an hour and a half if traffic is running smoothly to cross over the Indiana border on Interstate 90. Rick drives his Ford rental car with accelerated speed and heads for Valparaiso – namely the Porter County Sheriff's Office.

As Rick drives toward the Sheriff's Office located on State Road, he reflects on everything that has happened the past couple of weeks. He knows that he should be absolutely relieved and excited that he solved the serial murder case before there were more innocent victims. It's not over yet, and he knows that there will be more victims that he can't do anything about and that troubles him deeply. The plan is to head Donald off before there is more loss of life.

Fast moving rain clouds appear to be moving from the east and a few sprinkles mist the detective's windshield. He hopes that the weather holds just a little bit longer before the big storm strikes.

* * * * *

Just off the main street a white Toyota Camry is parked along the side of the road with a flat rear left tire. An elderly woman stands away from the road dressed in a raincoat waiting patiently. She pulls her coat tighter around her neck in anticipation of the imminent rain. A Sheriff's patrol car with the trunk open is parked behind the stranded vehicle. Sergeant Mike Sullivan has just retrieved a jack from his patrol car and is in the process of changing the flat tire. Road side service is backed up and will take at least two hours to respond, so the sergeant decided to take on the task personally.

Mike motions to the elderly woman. "Have a seat in the patrol car. It's going to pour any minute."

The elderly woman moves toward the police car relieved to be out of the weather. "Thank you." Mike makes sure she's safely in the passenger seat before he shuts the door.

Rick eases his rental car behind the police vehicle and parks. The Sheriff's Office advised him the sergeant's patrol area. He realizes that the stocky sergeant is preparing to change a tire. That was definitely not something that the Santa Cruz County Sheriff's Office would be seen doing – especially in the pouring rain.

The sky becomes darker and more ominous in preparation of a serious rainstorm by every passing minute. Rick zips up his leather jacket and turns up his collar. He opens his car door and walks toward the sergeant who is jacking up the car. He sees the woman seated in the patrol car anxiously waiting.

Rick stops ten feet from the sergeant and asks, "Sergeant Sullivan?"

Mike stands up and faces Rick. "What can I do for you?" He scrutinizes Rick and instantly sums up that he's not from Valparaiso or any surrounding big city in the area.

Rick continues, "I'm Rick Lopez, actually Detective Rick Lopez from the Santa Cruz Sheriff's Office in California. I'm trying to track down Emily Stone." He waits expectantly as the sergeant regards him cautiously.

"Well Detective Rick Lopez of the Santa Cruz

Sheriff's Office in California, can you change a tire?"

"What?" Rick couldn't believe what he just heard from the sergeant.

"Can you change a tire?"

"Well sure but."

"Good." He hands Rick the tire iron. "You'd better get moving before the storm hits."

Rick didn't want to discourage the sergeant from giving him any information, so he takes the tire iron and begins loosening the lug nuts on the wheel. The fine mist begins to turn to a light consistent rain making the tire iron slippery and unwieldy in the detective's hands.

Mike asks, "What makes you think that Emily Stone is here?"

Rick stops for a moment. "A hunch."

"Keep working." He makes a gesture in the air for Rick to keep twisting the tire iron. "You California detectives get a lot of hunches?"

Rick had no other choice, but to play along. "Sometimes. And sometimes we actually solve a case or two."

"Ah, but how often do you really get your hands dirty assisting the public?"

Rick finishes the last lug nut. "Obviously not often enough." He notices the sergeant's shirt is untucked and there's grease on his left pant leg.

Mike takes the spare tire out of the Camry's trunk and rolls it toward the detective. It now begins to rain. He then takes the old tire and puts it into the trunk.

For a moment or two, both police officers stare at one another in a law enforcement, different jurisdiction, cop standoff. Rick is beginning to get really wet and uncomfortable. He can feel the rain soaking through his shoes.

Mike finally breaks the silence, "Well, I'd suggest that you hurry up with that tire before you catch pneumonia."

Rick can't believe he let himself be hustled like this, but he begins to tighten down the lug nuts. His hands slip from the tire iron a few times and mud splatters across his face and chest. He grumbles and finishes the job as quickly as he can. Rick is soaking wet with mud covering the front of him. He begins to wipe his face and hands as best as he can under the circumstances. He starts to walk back to his car.

Mike yells to him, "Wait a minute, follow me into town."

Rick gets back into his rental car and quickly turns the car on and blasts the heat. He's freezing and hungry. He looks in the rearview mirror and is irritated by how he looks with several mud splats on the left side of his face. The rain begins to pick up momentum and begins to pour down. He watches for a moment as the sergeant helps the elderly woman back into her Camry.

Finally Mike pulls away from the side of the road and heads into town a mile away. The sergeant parks in front of a pizza and sandwich restaurant, and doesn't bother to wait for the detective. He continues inside and seats himself in a warm comfortable booth. Rick joins the sergeant and takes a seat in the booth across from him. Mike takes his time looking over the menu, but it's obvious that he's been to this restaurant a million times before.

Rick states, "Sergeant I'm really in a hurry; can you tell me if Emily is here in town?"

Mike looks up from his menu just as the waitress arrives and he places his order for a club sandwich with extra French fries. He continues, "And the California detective would like?"

Rick replies, "I'll have the same, thank you."

Mike turns his attention back to Rick and decides to continue his fun. "So what was it that you needed?"

Rick realizes that he is the focus of a small town police department practical joke. "How long are you going to have your fun?"

"As long as you let me."

"I'm a friend of Emily's. Is she here or not?"

The sergeant smiles and waits a moment for dramatic effect, "Yes, she's here."

Rick feels elated and is glad that he trusted his gut instinct. "Where?"

"I'd imagine she's probably sleeping right now; she was pretty exhausted when she arrived."

Rick knew he wasn't going to get anywhere with the sergeant until he was supposed to know.

The waitress brings their sandwiches.

The sergeant takes a big bite of the triple-decker

sandwich and mayonnaise oozes out the other side and spots the front of his uniform.

Rick prods, "I know if you call her, she'll say she knows me."

The sergeant says between bites, "I know who you are."

The two police officers eat in silence. Each is sizing the other up in their own suspicious way.

Rick persists, "Can you tell me why Emily left the Sheriff's Office?"

Mike is intrigued by the question; he thought that Emily might have told him why she quit.

Rick mumbles to himself while eating a French fry. "No, I suppose if you were going to tell me I'd have to tune up your car first."

The sergeant becomes serious for the first time since meeting Rick. "Did you hear about those officers who were arrested some years back for an organized rape ring?"

Rick accessed his memory and remembers some type of rape and assault that police officers were involved in about seven years ago. "Yes."

"Well, it's not something that we like to talk about around here. It's still real touchy to most. The department took a huge hit for the behavior of those nine officer's inexcusable behavior." The sergeant squirts more ketchup on his plate. "Who knows how long that would have gone on if one deputy hadn't come forward with what they knew."

Rick is quiet and allows the sergeant to continue.

"It was the most difficult decision that one person should have to carry."

"Emily found out which officers were committing those crimes and she came forward", Rick stated.

"She was the only female officer at the department at the time. And it was already very difficult for her, she was too smart and capable for her own good. And there were many who just didn't like it." The sergeant looks pained as he continues, "She first came to me for my advice."

"She sacrificed her career to do the right thing."

"That's Emily, she only sees right or wrong, no grey. But unfortunately, she got death threats and constant harassment, so she left town until everything blew over."

Rick reflects on the new information.

"Are you going to eat the rest of your fries?" The sergeant asks.

"No, go ahead." Rick pushes his half eaten sandwich and fries over to the sergeant.

Mike asks in complete seriousness as he munches on the fries, "So what are we going to do about your serial killer that's on his way here to kill her?"

Chapter 51
Saturday 1300 Hours

After driving almost seven hundred miles from Sacramento, Donald decides to look for a place to pull off in Utah. He sees the town of Wanship only a few miles ahead that overlooks the picturesque Weber River. He takes the only town exit and pulls into the gas station. He pumps gas while the Accomplice gets out and stretches his legs and back muscles.

The Accomplice looks around at the vast land and forest areas; he can't help but feel a new surge of killing adrenaline through his body. "What a perfect place for a ritual killing", he ponders. He observes a female hitchhiker that just left the gas station with a heavy backpack. The next kill should be something more extravagant than the last, he imagines.

Instead of driving back onto Interstate 80, Donald and the Accomplice decide to go sightseeing first. Donald pulls the car up next to the hitchhiker and rolls down the window.

"Hi, you going very far?" He asks.

The young redhead turns to study the two men, "Just to the next town."

"Do you know this area at all?"

She smiles, "Sure do."

"We wanted to do some light hiking and see the river. Do you know a guide around here?"

The hitchhiker thinks for a moment before answering. "I can take you there, if you can give me a ride to the next town afterwards."

"No problem, get in."

The hitchhiker gets in and tosses her backpack to the other side of the back seat. She climbs in and says, "Hi, I'm Rebecca."

Donald drives away slowly almost unable to contain his compulsion to smash her face in right there at the gas station. "Nice to meet you Rebecca", he replies.

* * * * *

The Mysterious Trail forks at the Weber River with a mixed forest of Aspen groves. There are wild strawberries growing everywhere and a scent of wild flowers is prominent in the fresh air. It would be a perfect place for a day hike and picnic. But today the forest is the perfect backdrop for a brutal murder. Donald and the Accomplice step from a grove of Aspen trees where the grisly remains of Rebecca lay exposed to the natural environment. She didn't know her fate until they pulled up to the parking area of the hiking trail, where she surrendered to unconsciousness from a quick blow to the face. Her limp body became the fertile grounds for the next escalation of horror.

Feeling energized with the intense killing high, Donald and the Accomplice get back into the car and find their way back to Interstate 90 through a scenic drive. The Killers are coming.

Chapter 52
Saturday 1630 Hours

Rick follows Mike in his rental car through a residential area where every yard is perfectly manicured and extremely tidy. Each home seems to exude the proud and hospitable quality of the entire town. There are many homes trimmed with brick surrounded by lush green lawns. Finally, Mike pulls his patrol vehicle next to a nice duplex and parks.

Rick has been extremely focused on finding Emily, but now that he's parked in front of the residence where she is staying, he feels a little bit nervous. He begins to think that maybe he's made a mistake. It would be awkward if Emily didn't want to see him after the long journey to get here. He now begins to feel embarrassed at his hasty decision to fly to Indiana. He definitely feels out of his comfort zone, unable to make a sound decision at the moment.

Mike exits his patrol car and begins to walk up the pathway to the front door of the duplex. He hesitates for a moment to wait for Rick to catch up with him. Rick follows his example and approaches the front door. Before either officer has the opportunity to knock, the door opens wide and Emily steps out to greet them.

Emily greets Rick first with a long hug. "I'm so glad to see you." She whispers in his ear, "I'm so glad you're here now."

Rick conveys, "You didn't think I'd let you get away that easily?"

Mike regards the couple and instantly sees their strong connection to one another. Whatever uncertainty he initially had about the California detective has just disappeared.

Mike temporarily breaks up the reunion, "Don't just stand out here yammering on, lets go inside."

Emily a bit embarrassed says, "Of course, please come in."

The three them go inside the duplex.

Rick realizes that the duplex is being refurbished for the most part, but it's still quite livable in the mean time. The windows, interior doors, and fixtures have been replaced.

Rick asks the sergeant, "You own this place?"

"Yup. I'm trying to update it a bit before I rent it out or possibly sell it in year or so."

Emily returns from the kitchen with a tray of iced tea and three glasses. "I thought you both might be thirsty."

Mike laughs to himself and says, "I think Detective Rick here has had enough liquid for awhile."

Emily watches the interaction between Rick and Mike. She realizes that she's missing something, but glad that they are getting along. She grabs Rick's hand and sits down on the couch with him. Mike takes his place in an old worn out armchair. There's an awkward silence as they stare at one another drinking iced tea. Rick updates Emily and Mike about everything that has transpired in the serial killer case with the identification of Donald Everett and the long drawn out hunt ending with the fingerprint and blood evidence. He further tells them about the body parts he had in his garage.

They sit in silence trying to get their minds wrapped around the current events.

Emily begins, "Well?"

Mike interrupts her, "I think we need to figure out what do when the killer gets to town."

Rick replies, "You mean set a trap?"

"That's not a bad idea."

Emily retorts, "What a minute. This town isn't, shall we say, used to psycho serial killers."

Rick asks, "What kind of special weapons and

tactics training do you have here?"

Slowly, Mike replies, "Well, we have four SWAT officers."

Rick pushes, "And?"

"They've had training initially when they took the positions a few years ago."

Rick thinks about the crime scenes he's witnessed and how cunning the killer is at surprising his victims.

Emily conveys, "We don't actually know yet if he is really coming after me."

"He is." Rick states matter of fact. "There was evidence in his house to substantiate that he's indeed coming after you. He thinks you're the reason why his life is so screwed up."

Mike adds, "Everything I've studied and read about these types of killers seems to indicate he's coming for you Emily. He's focused on the one person who has interrupted his freedom and killing. And he won't stop until he finds you."

"It's only a matter of time before he ends up here." Rick tries to sound upbeat, but in actuality it's killing him to know that this predator is now hunting Emily.

Emily says, "Maybe I should go somewhere else?" She looks down at her hands unable to meet their gaze.

"Absolutely not. It's going to stop now. We can't let this killer roam around free any longer; there are too many chances for more innocent victims." The sergeant states adamantly.

"I agree", Rick replies.

The three begin to formulate a plan to trap Donald.

Emily finally comes clean and explains her interaction with Donald before she left town. She tells them about the attack in the middle of the night, the face-to-face meeting, trapped inside the building in Pajaro, and her attack on him in his house.

Rick watches Emily as she recounts her harrowing stories and he can't believe that this petite woman could fight with such vengeance.

Emily says, "I know it was wrong to go to his house and threaten him, but I didn't really know he was the serial killer."

Mike defends her position, "It doesn't matter now; everything's finally out in the open."

Rick adds, "We have to set a trap so he thinks that he's actually going to get to Emily."

"My men are at your disposal for whatever you need."

Rick continues, "Unfortunately we're going to need a lot of preparation and some training. Can I count on you to lead them?"

"Absolutely."

Rick was involved in SWAT training early in his career, but this town hasn't seen any type of action to support such law enforcement activities. He worries about the capability and dedication of the officers.

Mike continues, "I have some ideas as to how to make Emily seem easily visible in town where this killer can follow the clues right to us."

"I don't mind being the bait. It's the only way it'll work." Emily adds.

Both officers answer her at the same time, "No way."

"We have time to coordinate this sting without you ever having any contact with him." Mike sits up straighter in his chair and finishes the last of his iced tea. He begins, "This is my idea."

Chapter 53
Saturday 2200 Hours

Donald and the Accomplice ride in silence as they cross the border into the state of Wyoming. Donald then eases the car onto Interstate 25 going south toward Colorado. He is alert and in high spirits for the first time in many months. He is gaining momentum with the important task at hand and the impending excitement causes the nerves in his body to tingle with a slight vibration. He has never felt quite like this before; usually after a kill he slowly begins to feel let down. Now he is undeniably ready for Emily and his transition to the ultimate freedom, but he will have to support his high energy along the way with a few more sacrificial victims.

The Accomplice wrestles with his own thoughts and feelings as he rides next to Donald in silence. He muses that his ultimate contribution to society will forever be branded in history and the public will not soon forget his mastery. His strength and power will live on long after he has left this earth. He has no doubt that he will be reincarnated as the most stealthy and feared hunter. The killing of Emily will clinch this commitment. He watches casually the picturesque scenery move by the passenger window and wonders if Donald is thinking about the next sacrifice too.

Donald eases the car off the Interstate a good thirty miles before the city of Denver. The land is vast and green, but everything looks dark and bleak at this late evening hour. Earlier, the Rocky Mountains had looked more like a postcard you send home to friends and family instead of what is outside the perceptions of the car windshield. The gravel road doesn't appear to have a road sign or a town name, but it doesn't matter. The point of interest is the poor dilapidated trailer park scattered with a few dwellings and abandoned cars about a mile ahead.

The Accomplice still remains quiet and stares straight ahead, but his intense excitement is escalating. This wonderful element of surprise makes the act of the kill that much more pleasurable. He never asks where they are going; it would only cheapen the experience. He sees a small sign that reads, "Bear Creek Park". Nothing looks like there are any bears for a hundred miles or more. The name was obviously a leftover from the Indians and would only possess any type of importance to them in historical times.

Donald drives through the makeshift trailer park and heads toward a small trailer at the end illuminated with a tiny outside light. He could wait in the car to see if there is possibly more than one woman inside, but he's anxious and doesn't want to wait. The Accomplice must have read his mind; he turns and gets a .38 revolver from the back seat. It was perfect. Everything was perfect. The scene has been set. If there was another unsuspecting person or if someone else came home at this late hour, they would be dead before they knew what happened.

The Killers get out of their car and walk straight to the trailer. The trailer which is partially hidden from view by trees and the evening. The Accomplice places the gun in his waistband. The doorway had some handcrafted ornaments with a dream catcher fluttering in the wind. A soft wind chime could be heard in the distance as they walked to the front entrance.

Within a second, the Accomplice kicks in the flimsy front door. The Killers ascend on the trailer like storm troopers, and it takes them only two seconds to find a startled woman in her mid-thirties with long dark hair. She sits straight up in bed with a startled expression but not before the Accomplice incapacitated her with several expert blows to the face.

Donald goes to the kitchen to find anything of interest in the refrigerator. He takes a look around the trailer and is satisfied that no one is going to interrupt them. He can hear the Accomplice terrorizing the woman in and out of consciousness. The sound of his awaiting freedom is getting closer with every last breath of the dying woman. He drinks a cherry soda patiently waiting for his time as the fierce hunter pouncing upon his prey.

The Killers are coming.

Chapter 54
Sunday 0900 Hours

The previous small workout studio now incorporates the designated training area for the Porter County Sheriff's Office. It is an improvised gym that is generally used for police officers that want to work out with weights, treadmills, and heavy weight punching bags. The basement of the building has integrated a private gun shooting range with six available lanes. Officers can practice for their firearm recertification.

There are eight off-duty police officers mulling

around the gym waiting for Sergeant Sullivan to arrive. Most officers are dressed in sweats and t-shirts; some are casually lifting free weights killing time. A couple of men are conversing about the recent events and the possible excitement that might hit their small sleepy town.

Mike arrives wearing a loose fitting jogging suit and promptly updates the officers to the situation and what he expects from them.

"Listen up." The sergeant waits a moment before he continues, "If there is anyone here who doesn't want to be a part of this you can leave now. And you won't be faulted in any way for your decision not to participate."

The group looks around, but no one makes a move to leave the room.

Rick enters the gym carrying a couple of manila file folders.

Mike nods at Rick as he joins him. "Okay, this is Detective Rick Lopez from the Santa Cruz Sheriff's Office in California. He is going to be working with you individually with special weapons and tactics."

Rick nods his introduction to the eager group. He can't help but notice that these men seem extremely young and would seem more suited for working farms rather than setting a trap for a ruthless serial killer.

Mike turns to Rick, "Okay, Rick will fill you in on some details."

Rick begins, "The man we will be setting up for

surveillance and capture is Donald Everett." He opens the folder and hands out vital statistics on Donald and recent photos of him and his possible vehicles to the police officers. "Make no mistake by his chubby and ordinary appearance. He has a genius I.Q. and is extremely dangerous. He has already tortured, killed, and dismembered four women we know of, and he's on his way here for one reason only - to kill."

Raising his hand, one of the officers asks, "Sir?"

Rick responds, "Yes."

The officer asks, "How do you know when he'll arrive?"

"It will take as long it takes for him to drive here from California." Rick looks at his watch, "A little less than twenty hours if we're lucky."

The sergeant interjects, "The way this is going to work is that we are going to conduct intelligence around town. Each group will watch the main roads, motels, and diners." He looks to Rick.

Rick continues, "He's methodical and predictable in his killing work. He will systematically search for his victim through intelligence and organization. We will be there waiting for him to take the bait. Basically, we will be leaving a trail of breadcrumbs for him to follow." Rick looks around at the group, worried about their skills for the special assignment. "I will update each group individually as to their specific assignments."

Sergeant Sullivan steps up, "Alright everyone pair off, two groups stay here with Rick and the others come with me to the firing range."

The officers pair off and wait for their assignments. Rick approaches the sergeant before he leaves to go to the firing range.

"Do you think these men have what it takes?" Rick asks.

"One thing you need to realize is that everyone here takes their job and the safety of the citizens very seriously."

"Because we don't have any other choice. We can't afford to be wrong, and I'm not going to let anything happen to Emily."

Mike adds, "Don't worry about these boys; they have heart as well as ability."

"Okay." Rick joins his two teams in the gym.

Mike waits a moment and watches Rick explain basic tactics to the young men. The sergeant not only worries about the impact of the situation on the officers, but the impact on the community if something goes terribly wrong.

Chapter 55
Sunday 1300 Hours

D onald and the Accomplice have just finished lunch at a small greasy diner somewhere in Nebraska territory just off Interstate 76. They will be passing over the border into the state of Iowa soon. For the past four hundred miles both men have said fewer than twenty words to one another, but it has proven to be obvious that they don't need to verbally communicate with each other in the conventional way. The synchronized behavior rituals more than make up the lack of conversation between the two killers. It is almost as if they were separated at birth as twins and now they have found each other again by a macabre twist of fate. It's that fate that drives their compulsions to kill, each for individual requirements of their psyche, but the Killer Twins have more in common than they realize.

The two men from completely different backgrounds met by accident during a trolling expedition. They gravitated toward one another in an almost hypnotic trance that has endured the test of time. After their first kill more than a year ago, the relationship was finalized forever. If one were to die unexpectedly, the other would be lost in the world of murder and torture. The kills wouldn't mean as much or be as fulfilling as in the past without their murder life partner. In order to get to the next level and keep the killing phases moving forward in a chronological order, they must kill each time with a new heightened sense of urgency as well as the use of pure, terrifying ingenuity.

Donald is hypnotized by the rushing countryside he sees through the windshield and the hum of the engine cruising at a comfortable eighty-five miles per hour. He knows that he is gaining momentum before his meeting with Emily because his cells, nerves, veins, and blood alerts every pore in his body that he's ready. It contributes to an extraordinary murder high.

The wonderful road trip experiences have surpassed Donald's expectations as a prerequisite until his final kill. It is the essential power and autonomy that he craves more than a breath of air. The need propels forward, and eventually it will lead him to his final freedom for everyone to witness. He casually looks over at the Accomplice and references his posture and escalating energy level as well. It's time again to feed the dark monster that lurks just beneath the surface of flesh and bone. They have driven past signs that alert drivers to the upcoming exits of Des Moines. It sounds like as good a place as any to troll for the next victim. Donald takes the next exit.

The Accomplice turns to Donald and says, "Good choice." He relishes the memories of when he told Donald of his big secret a little over a year ago. His fantasies just keep getting bigger and better. Donald acknowledges him and continues to an unknown destination. Sometimes it amazed him how in tune they were to one another; they are indeed the two absolute sections to one whole mortal person.

Donald drives through an older part of town and systematically takes each street in order. There are many old abandoned buildings where junkies and other deviants hang out in dark doorways until their next fix. Some suspiciously regard Donald and the Accomplice driving slowly through the forgotten neighborhoods, but quickly disregard them as cops or other deviants.

Several street prostitutes carefully watch the slow vehicle and make a few enticing comments to try to get them to stop. Donald continues to drive past the first three women. The car turns the corner and accelerates slightly down an alley. Before the car makes another systematic turn, he notices a pale petite brunette extinguishing a cigarette.

Donald slows and then stops the car. He rolls down the window, "Need a ride?"

Smiling and walking toward the car, "Sure baby, anything you say."

Donald smiles. "Get in."

The young woman swiftly gets into the back seat and they slowly drive away.

The Killers are coming.

Chapter 56
Sunday 1900 Hours

E mily and Rick are seated at a quiet booth in a Japanese Restaurant sipping sake. Most of their sushi has been delightfully eaten, only a few pieces remaining on their plates.

"This is a nice restaurant." Rick politely states.

Looking around, Emily replied, "Yes, it is."

Rick absently eats the last piece of sushi on his plate. "You just can't eat just one." He laughs.

"I agree." She smiles. "You should never waste a good piece of sushi."

For the first time since he laid eyes on her, Rick

observes now that Emily is relaxed and at ease. It was far different than the frantic and intense woman he met earlier. She smiles with a gleam in her eye as she chats about what it was like growing up in Indiana and the wonderful summers that she never wanted to have end. She talks about the warm summer nights where you could stay out all night and the incredible starry skies where her world seemed galaxies away. She fantasized about all of the things she would do with her life.

Rick tells Emily of his childhood in Oakland and San Francisco in a somewhat gentler time. He had it tough in a poor neighborhood, but his parents always made sure that he had the necessities. He had begun to run with some bad kids in his teens, but the intervention of a caring police officer helped to change his destiny and shape the person he's become today.

Rick explains, "I remember when this police officer really got my attention and sat me down."

"I bet you remember his name." Emily adds.

"Officer Christopher Lewis."

"See, I knew it."

"He died a couple of years later in liquor store robbery." He pauses. "That's when I definitely knew I wanted to be a cop. What about you?"

"Me?"

"Every cop has a story about why he became a cop."

"I had a childhood friend that I had known since Kindergarten, Pam. She had nice parents and a great house where I played often, but one day something went terribly wrong."

Rick listens and watches Emily's body language change from strong to fragile.

"There were many conflicting stories, but it still didn't change the outcome. Pam's dad shot her mom and then turned the gun on himself. Luckily Pam wasn't there at the time."

"That's terrible."

"It was, but what I really remember the most were the police officers. It was the way they handled the scene; you could really see the anguish on their faces, but they took care of everyone else first. They were selfless." Emily takes another sip of sake. "I remember I wanted to be strong and look after the neighborhood the way they did."

Rick and Emily sit quietly each lost in thought, but it was not an awkward silence. The realization of the many things they have in common was extremely real at the moment.

Emily is the first to speak again, "Well."

Rick smiles and replies, "Let's get out of here."

"Sounds good."

As Rick pays the check, Emily waits out in the parking lot. She muses that it's always about a killer or child abductor. Her whole life has been consumed with the hunt of the next serial killer. Now, perhaps, she has the opportunity to have a normal life and be happy with someone.

Rick sneaks up behind her, "You lost?" He slips his arms around her waist.

Emily laughs, "I guess maybe I am."

Rick sneaks a couple of kisses from Emily. He asks, "What's there to do around this town anyway?"

"Wow, I actually have some time off for a change too. Let me see." She smiles at Rick. "I know. You game?"

"You bet."

Emily instructs Rick to drive to a far area of town where a picturesque park is located. There are an abundance of trees and a man made lake. The water sparkles in the early evening dusk. A paved walking trail winds around the lake adorned with colorful flowers and shrubbery. There are benches every fifty feet to rest or to just enjoy the tranquil view. There's a sense of peace and tranquility that illuminates the landscape.

Emily adds, "I know it's not exciting, but it's the closest thing I could think of to like walking at the beach."

"It's nice. I don't think I've slowed down enough lately to just enjoy nature."

"Well, I figured it was definitely something that we both could do that didn't entail grisly crime scene photos and serial killers."

Rick taunts, "I think there's at least one other thing we could do together that doesn't include serial killers."

"That's my back up plan." Emily laughs.

Emily grabs Rick's hand and leads him down a pathway that interconnects around the lake. She takes him off the regular walkway and through an overgrown path on the south end of the lake. She seems to know it well. It's deserted and there's a small rickety boat landing nestled in the trees that ends at the lake. It reveals a private swimming section. Emily kicks her shoes off, strips her t-shirt off, and begins unbuttoning her jeans.

Rick asks surprised, "What are you doing?"

"What does it look like? You are a detective, right?" She teases.

Before Rick can respond, Emily has stripped down to her bra and panties.

Emily continues, "I don't know about you, but I'm going to cool off from this humidity." She jumps into the lake with a splash and disappears under the water.

The cool water feels incredible on her skin. Emily dives under the water again until her lungs could no longer exhale. She feels alive and revived by the water with an almost invincible energy. The outdoor air now feels cool instead of humid and hot. She looks back at the old boat landing, but Rick is nowhere in sight. She was so lost in her own thoughts that she didn't see where he went.

Now Emily begins to swim back to the dock; still no sign of Rick. She is about to hoist herself back onto the dock when she is pulled backward into the water. Rick grabs her around the waist and kisses her with passionate excitement.

Emily catches her breath, "I thought you ran away."

"You're going to have to do more than that to scare me away." Rick splashes her. "I take it you've done this before?"

"Just once." She pauses. "Okay, twice." Emily laughs and swims toward the other side of the lake followed closely by Rick.

Chapter 57
Monday 0600 Hours

The early sun has been up for about an hour and the afterglow of murder still lingers in Donald's mind and body. The terrified screams in his mind are only reminiscent of the kill, but the sweet salty taste of blood and flesh will forever be engrained in his memory to relive over and over again. He can feel himself getting closer to Emily, almost as if he could reach out and touch her at that exact moment. He will soon absorb her soul into his and reap the benefits of the final transition. No one will deny him again of power and strength - ever.

The last kill took longer than expected, but it was well worth it. The best is about to begin, the grand finale. Donald continues to drive along Interstate 80 toward Chicago and they are about a hundred and fifty miles before they reach the windy city.

Donald is growing tired of the same countryside for the last day, but his memories of victims keep his mind alert and content. His compulsion urges him to move forward with growing urgency. The more he thinks about Emily and her self-righteousness, the more he knows that his plan is perfect to snuff out her very existence and then absorb into his own.

A police siren jolts Donald back to reality. He looks in the rearview mirror and sees an Aurora police officer riding his bumper with sirens and lights directed at him. He can see a middle-aged man with a heavy mustache driving with intensity. Donald knows that he wasn't speeding at that moment, so the local Santa Cruz police must have connected him to the crime scenes and distributed his name and license plates as a wanted killer. He regards this escalating situation for a moment and then smiles. He looks to his Accomplice who confirms his thoughts and effortlessly tucks the gun under his right leg for easy retrieval.

Donald eases the car off the Interstate down a dirt access road to a water treatment facility. The area is deserted and offers some camouflage from prying eyes. Donald keeps the car slowly rolling another ten feet for good measure.

The Aurora police officer switches his sirens off but keeps the red and blue lights flashing. The officer carefully exits his vehicle with his standard issue firearm aimed right at Donald and the Accomplice. He has a steady hand and knows proper procedures, which indicates that he's a seasoned police officer.

From a routine license plate check, Aurora Police Officer Jenkins discovered that the car belongs to a wanted serial killer from California and is considered to be armed and extremely dangerous. The early day shift is actively developing into a front-page headline for him. Back up support is twenty minutes away, but the situation won't wait until help arrives.

Officer Jenkins moves cautiously toward the vehicle. He sees two individuals inside staring straight ahead. His mind searches the possibility of a hostage or hitchhiker that the killer picked up along the way. His adrenaline is pumping, but his hands are steady as a rock.

"Put your hands where I can see them! Now!"

Officer Jenkins watches the two seated men put their hands in the air.

"Driver get out of the vehicle with your hands up!"

Donald slowly opens the door and steps out with his hands in the air. He says innocently, "What seems to be the problem officer?"

"Shut up and keep your hands in the air. Turn around now."

Officer Jenkins moves in and quickly retrieves his handcuffs from his belt. He pushes Donald up against the hood and handcuffs his hands behind his back. He reaches into Donald's pocket and takes out his wallet with his California driver's license. "Well, well. Looks like somebody wants you real bad."

"I don't know what you're talking about officer." Donald says harmlessly.

To Donald, "Stay right there." Officer Jenkins walks around to the passenger side door. "Sir, are you okay?"

The Accomplice takes a big sigh of relief, "Thank you so much officer for saving my life. He's a mad man and was going to kill me."

"Do you have any identification?"

The Accomplice reaches slowly into his pocket and takes out his wallet. "Yes, I have my driver's license. Let me see, it's here somewhere." He then hands the officer his license.

Officer Jenkins reads aloud, "Mr. Leo Lewinski?"

"Yes?"

"Come with me."

"Just a moment, I need to get my backpack with my pills in it."

Officer Jenkins turns slightly and realizes that Leo was going to retrieve something beside the passenger seat. He made a fatal error in judgment and his instincts knew it before his mind. Before he can raise his firearm, a blast slams into his chest knocking him off of his feet. His gun falls to the ground. The searing heat in his chest makes the officer writhe in pain and try to get up, but another blast hits him square in the forehead. All sounds and colors go black permanently.

Leo grabs the officer's firearm and tosses it in the back seat of the car. He quickly riffles through the officer's keys and finds the handcuff key to release Donald.

Tossing the handcuffs on the ground, Donald orders, "Put him in the trunk."

Leo obediently drags the dead officer to the back of the police vehicle. He finds the correct key and opens the compartment. He heaves the body into the trunk and slams the lid down.

Donald and Leo return to their car and back out of the service road to the Interstate. Donald is thinking ahead, it was just a minor setback. They must now ditch the car and steal another one, but they should arrive in Valparaiso by 1500 hours. Emily will soon be theirs for the slaughter and life will truly begin.

The Killers are coming.

Chapter 58
Monday 0900 Hours

E mily and Rick enjoy a wonderful morning sleeping in late together. They spent most of the evening inseparable and praying the night would never end, making love and not thinking about the inevitable events of the approaching day. They both feel refreshed and energized for the first time in many years. It was a new beginning and a new day.

It was time for Rick to meet with Mike and the other volunteer officers to plan the exact details of their surveillance and eventual capture of Donald Everett.

Emily props herself up on a couple of pillows and watches Rick get dressed. "How are the boys doing?"

"I think they are going to be okay." Rick didn't want to worry Emily because he was afraid that she would do something on her own.

"That's good." She didn't completely believe him. His eyes were a dead giveaway.

Rick sits down on the bed and kisses Emily for a couple of minutes.

Emily stops and says, "You're going to be late."

"So I can be late."

"I'll see you a little later on." She smiles and stares into his eyes. "Don't worry, it'll be okay."

He takes one last look at the woman he knows that he's going to marry one day. "Alright, we'll meet back up with you later."

"Yes, sir." She makes a silly salute.

Within a few seconds, Rick is gone. Emily remains in bed for a few minutes trying to digest everything. Just when she thinks she had everything figured out in her life, along came Rick. She never thought that anyone like him would ever enter her life and completely understand her.

Emily throws back the bed sheets and heads into the bathroom to take a shower. It was her time to really think through her next move and she knew that it didn't include Rick, Mike, or the boys. The steam filling the shower stall helped to relax her nerves and clear her head. She had so much to lose, but now she had gained a whole new beginning once this incident was behind her.

With her hair still wet, Emily sits at her laptop computer in the kitchen and views several CDs that she copied from Donald's computer. She looks through his personal records of bank accounts, credit cards, and cell phone records. There's nothing interesting or unusual in the billing or financial records. She views some document and photo files. She opens the computer files that seem to coincide with dates and years. To her disbelief, she has found a killing log. The dates are much earlier than the first homicide in Santa Cruz. There's a notation that an appendage was removed from each victim. What's more disturbing is that there are more than a hundred entries of death in the spreadsheet. There are files that have crude depictions of death and dismemberment with some kind of bird in the upper left hand corner. The bird seems to be a higher source of power for Donald.

Emily spends about an hour putting all of the evidence together. She knows that Rick will be able to piece the clues to other homicides. She can't help but feel that there is another person who has been helping Donald. It's been bothering her for quite some time, especially with the attacks and the way the victims were tortured, killed, and then the staging of the crime scenes.

The evidence that Donald has so carefully maintained in the computer files has made up Emily's mind. The only way that she can truly be free from her turbulent past and keep Rick and the others safe from this unremitting monster is to trap him by herself. The only reason that he's coming to this wonderful town is because of her – pure and simple. By beating Donald at his own game is the only way that she can actually begin a new life. She will end this drama once and for all.

Emily knows deep in her bones that she must do this alone. She picks up her cell phone and punches in a text message. She hesitates for only a couple of seconds, and presses send.

Chapter 59
Monday 1130 Hours

Donald and Leo commandeered a brown Toyota pick up truck at a local strip mall for the rest of their journey. The truck won't be missed until some unsuspecting soul leaves work and finds it missing. It will buy the killers more time. It's not going to be long now, just a mere couple of hours left to the road trip.

Donald steers steadfastly along the Interstate 294 Express that will eventually turn into the Portions toll before crossing the state line into Indiana.

He is hungry for the hunt. He is famished. He is eager. It is reminiscent of the highflying Peregrine Falcon searching for its prey. He is the perfect and efficient hunting machine that is relentless in the search for blood and violence. Donald will be the only living human to make history and be totally free to fly with the falcons. He will be revered and terrified by those who have seen his destruction.

Leo tenses his muscles as he feels Donald's shared energy. He feels what Donald feels, and there isn't a law enforcement agency or force that can stop their momentum now. He has waited so long to complete his mission, and now Emily will complete him. It took every ounce of strength for him to refrain from killing her during one of her personal training appointments. It took more self-control than any mere mortal could endure, but he wasn't just any ordinary man. He has been given the supremacy to kill from a higher psychological power and he plans on carrying out this request at any cost.

The traffic slows a bit as the congestion begins to take over the lanes. Donald receives a distinct chime from his cell phone that alerts him to an incoming text message. He looks to his phone and punches a button to reveal a text message from Emily. He knew that his prey would eventually lead him to her, and now she knows the truth too. He absently runs his fingers over his hunting knife that he keeps next to him at all times.

The text message reads: *meet 1257 carr if u*

dare 2 b free

Donald looks at Leo and smiles. He didn't need to verbally explain to him what the message said, but Leo knew. Donald has found a new energy that he's never felt before. It was curious. It was fulfilling. He can feel his freedom and satisfaction. He replies to the text message with a simple: *c u there*

The Killers are coming.

Chapter 60
Monday 1300 Hours

Rick takes a break from working with four of the police officers at the gym on defensive tactics. Before he has a chance to sit down and drink some water, Mike bursts through the door.

"We've got a problem. Come with me", the sergeant barks at Rick.

Rick doesn't say a word and follows the sergeant out to his small Ford sport utility vehicle.

"I've been tracking anything unusual between here and California." He explains.

Mike opens the back passenger door where two laptop computers are hooked up to a wireless satellite for instant Internet access. One of the computer screens shows a map of the United States. There is a road in red that illustrates the driving route from California to Indiana. There are green dots at various places along the way.

"What does this mean?" Rick asks.

The sergeant begins, "This is the most direct route that Donald is taking to get here."

Rick studies the map. "What are the green dots?"

"They represent homicides coinciding with the timing of his driving route. I've calculated approximate driving time allowing for gas and food with the approximate times of deaths." The sergeant points to the cities of Sacramento, Wanship, Denver, Des Moines, and Aurora.

"There have been five victims along Interstate 80 within the last twenty or so hours. The news media has picked up the story and has dubbed him the I-80 Killer."

"When was the last murder?" Rick is beginning to grow alarmed. Donald has made exceptional driving time and Rick has underestimated his determination.

"They found an Aurora police officer in the trunk of his patrol car this morning. Apparently he ran the plates and it came back with a wanted fugitive."

Rick takes a step back trying to calculate in his

mind how long it would take to drive from Aurora to Valparaiso.

As if reading Rick's mind, the sergeant replies, "It would take about two hours or so to get here."

Rick asks, "When was the officer's body found?"

"About eleven this morning."

Rick looks at his watch, "He could already be here. I've got to get Emily."

Mike shuts the car door. "You get Emily and I'll get the men in place." Further he states, "Check back in on the cell in half an hour."

Rick nods and rushes to his rental car. It was down to the wire and they may have just run out of time.

Chapter 61
Monday 1330 Hours

Rick storms through the front door of the duplex desperately looking for Emily. "Emily?" There was no answer. He looks in the bedroom and bathroom. Emily is nowhere to be found. He notices that she was working on her computer in the kitchen and also finds that her small duffle bag is gone. He knows that she carries two Glocks and extra clips in that bag. Suddenly, with imminent dread, he realizes that she went out alone to catch Donald. "No Emily", he says under his breath.

He is truly scared for the first time in his life because now his life seems to make perfect sense. When he walks back by the bedroom he sees a note on the pillow that Emily left him. He quickly clutches it in his hand, not wanting to read it right away because he knows what it will say.

With all of his physical strength, Rick unfolds the piece of paper and it reads: *I'm sorry, but I can't take the chance that someone else will get killed because of me. I can't lose you now. This will all be over soon. E*

Rick stands still unable to move; his legs are frozen like a stone statue. He knows that he would do exactly the same thing in the same situation. That's why they are so compatible and seem at ease with one another. Emily's drive and commitment keeps her going to do the right thing. He loves her because of it, but now he's absolutely terrified for her safety.

Holding his emotions in check, Rick dials his cell phone.

* * * * *

Mike has given the last instructions to the specialized teams. The four teams are going to cover four separate areas of the town each supplied with all of the appropriate weapons and electronic equipment. He and Rick will watch various establishments such as the motels and diners with the computer software surveillance that he designed.

The teams disperse to their locations. The sergeant walks to his car when his cell phone rings.

He pushes the send button and says, "Sullivan." It was Rick calling him early and he sounded distressed.

Rick blurts out, "Emily is gone, and she's going to try and catch this guy on her own."

"What?"

"You know Emily, she wants everyone to be safe. She thinks this is all her fault." Rick could barely catch his breath.

"Stay right there, I'll come and pick you up." He presses the end button on the cell phone.

Mike can't say that he was surprised by Emily's impulsive behavior, but now the stakes have doubled or even tripled. And the odds were not good.

Chapter 62
Monday 1400 Hours

E mily lingers in the shadows of the old musty warehouse listening to every sound both real and imagined. Her fear has turned to borderline terror as she continues to wait for Donald to arrive. The safety has been disengaged from her weapon and her anxious energy has caused her thumb to constantly fidget with the gun's mechanisms. She has managed to hide the other Glock in a safe hiding place in a storage closet and positioned some metal bars around the warehouse for quick retrieval if self-defense tactics are needed.

Her blood pounds annoyingly in her ears, and her heart rate increases a beat with every passing minute. She tries to steady her nerves by breathing slowly in and out, but it doesn't seem to help. When she dares to close her eyes she sees Rick's smiling face and his strong body. She counts the moments until she can be reunited with him again.

The musty smell of the area around her seems to be getting stronger and more pungent than when she first arrived. She continues to check every possible entry into the warehouse because she can't afford any surprises. She made sure that every entrance was blocked except for the door that she wanted Donald to enter. She set a trap with barbed wire and jagged steel on the two windows that were accessible. The musty smell of a closed utility space of mechanical grease and industrial cleaning agents is beginning to make Emily nauseous and a little bit dizzy. Her balance seems to be slightly affected by the toxic mixture.

Emily paces from each secure dark corner to the next, waiting in anticipation. She realizes that her epiphany is everything that she has experienced in her life and has led up to this exact moment in time. With that understanding, she begins to feel more relaxed and almost at eternal peace. She's not scared anymore, even though her life may be a stake. Her pulse rate and anxiety levels begin to lessen. Her breathing pattern becomes calm and even. She continues to wait; it will only be a matter of minutes before she can put everything behind her and move forward.

She sits down on a dusty crate and intently listens to any sounds coming from the perimeter of the building. There's a loud crash on the east side of the building. A window has been smashed and shattered glass shards spray into the gloomy building.

* * * * *

Mike screeches to a stop in front of the duplex and jumps out of the SUV barely able to set the emergency brake. Within seconds, Rick meets him at the doorway. Mike notices that Rick seems to be to the point of frantic, unlike the strong and intelligent detective he initially met in the rain.

The sergeant blurts out, "Any news?"

"No, but she took her two extra weapons."

"She means business, and she won't resurface until it's all over." Mike brushes past Rick and goes into the house. He opens her notebook computer on the kitchen table and begins to search through visited files.

Rick asks, "What are you doing?"

"I'm trying to see what she was looking at that made her act alone."

"From her computer?"

Mike explains, "You see, Emily's being systematic and she will look at all angles before she makes a final decision."

"That's why she was so effective with hunting

down child abductors." Rick watches as the sergeant scrolls through files.

"Exactly. She's extremely analytical." He shakes his head. "It looks like she was looking at files from another source. A CD or back up drive."

Rick recalls his memory of Donald's house. "There were computer files at Donald's house. Remember, Emily said that she copied some of his files."

The sergeant adds, "She must've found something on them."

"There must've been more information about the victims. But why would she do this alone?"

Mike looks directly at Rick. "That's what Emily has been doing her entire life – handling these types of situations alone."

Rick looks at a phone number on a piece of paper. "That's a cell number for the Santa Cruz area."

"That's how she's able to contact him in order to direct him exactly where she wants. She called him on the cell or sent a text message."

Rick responds, "We may already be too late."

Chapter 63
Monday 1415 Hours

Looking for anything that shifts within the darkness, Emily moves stealthily toward the broken window with her weapon targeted ahead of her. As she eases closer, her foot kicks a rock on the floor. She quickly examines the rock, kicks it out of her way, and surmises that someone must have thrown the rock through the window on purpose. It was either to scare Emily or act as a diversion to sneak into the warehouse.

Donald is close; Emily can almost feel him breathing on the back of her neck. She backs away from the broken window and retreats into the shadows once again to wait before her next move. She stares at a far western corner of the warehouse where the shadows are thick and appear to be moving. The more she stares at the dark corners, the more sinister the shadows become. She curses herself silently for not remembering to bring a flashlight, but it would only act as a bright beacon to direct Donald right to her.

Emily blinks twice and notices that the shadows have changed again. It seems that they have shape shifted into another creature. This time the shadow transforms into a human form of evil. Donald walks toward her out of the shadows reborn from the depths of darkness. He sees her but doesn't fear her conventional weapon.

Emily steps from her shadow cover and aims the firearm directly at Donald. "Stay right there. Don't move."

"You're not going to shoot me." Donald smiles wickedly and licks his lips.

"And what planet are you from?"

"I have the answers you so desperately have searched for your entire life." He stops and stares at her wanting to rip her neck from her shoulders to reveal blood and bone.

"I don't care about your psychotic delusions." She touches her cell phone that is attached to her belt. It gives a couple of distinct beeps alerting her that no signal is available.

Donald smiles wider, "No signal?" He is clearly

enjoying the cat and mouse repartee.

"Get down on the ground now!" She takes a couple of steps toward him.

Donald obeys and slowly drops to his knees. "You don't want to hear what I have to say?" His black eyes pierce through her soul with the intensity of an aggressive bird of prey.

"About how screwed up your life was as a child and how you can't stand women in authority and that's why you're driven to kill? I don't think so."

Donald moves into a praying stance with his palms together and continues, "Did you know that your parents didn't have to die?"

Emily stops.

Donald could see that he had hit a very delicate nerve with her. "I know who killed them and why."

"There's no way you could know."

"I know that the only thing that was stolen was your mother's wedding ring." He reaches into his pocket slowly and retrieves a wedding ring. He tosses it toward Emily. "Go ahead read the inscription." He recites it with a dramatic flair, "My one and only true love. How quaint."

Emily feels like she was struck by a cement truck and then run over by a runaway train. Her heart aches and her stomach feels overwhelmingly acid. No one knew about her mother's ring.

Donald laughs, and it echoes eerily through the warehouse. "So I've got your attention now?"

Emily tries to maintain her authority. "But how?"

Interrupting Emily, he says, "How do I know? Because I heard it straight from the killer's mouth."

Emily relaxes her arm muscles just for a moment to regain her composure, when a physically powerful force grabs her from behind. She's in a bear hug and can't seem to catch her breath, but she manages to hold onto the gun. She squeezes a couple of rounds off causing them to ricochet off of the cement walls but missing any intended target.

Emily could hear Donald laughing across the room as she struggles to free herself from an unknown assailant. The unknown perpetrator easily picks her up and slams her face down on the floor. The gun clatters out of her hand and skids across the room into the shadows. Her shoulders and chest are burning and she can feel the salty liquid that her lip and gums are bleeding. She gasps but her lungs are empty.

The perpetrator yanks her to her feet and holds her right arm taunt just before the breaking point. Emily turns to face her attacker and can't believe that she's staring into the face of Leo her personal trainer.

Barely able to breath, Emily says, "Leo?"

"I've waited your whole life for this moment to finish the job." Leo exclaims with enthusiasm. "You see my first kill was suppose to be a family and you weren't there. I've tracked you down all these years later and waited for the perfect moment to complete my first kill. All of the others don't count until you're dead. Don't you see?" He looks at Emily with contempt and love at the same time. "Don't you see why I have to do this?"

* * * * *

Rick is seated behind the wheel of the sergeant's car driving through town looking at every pedestrian's face. Mike is checking in on the radio with the other officers, but there have been no visuals on Donald or Emily.

Rick says, "Where is Emily? She couldn't have just disappeared. You know her, and you know this town. Where would she have gone? Think!"

Mike is frustrated too, but he keeps going over in his mind where she would have directed this killer. He says, "It has to be a place where she knows the layout well and away from any innocent bystanders."

Rick takes a hard turn and says, "What about buildings, storage facilities, or warehouses? Anything out of town or under construction?"

"Of course." Mike realizes exactly where she would have gone. "How could I be so stupid?"

"Where?"

"There's a building just outside of town that used to be the training facility for the Porter County Sheriff's Office."

"Which way?"

"Take a right here."

Rick cranks a hard right and continues driving fast.

Mike explains, "It's a big processing plant that was closed down thirty years ago, and then the county took it over for training purposes. About five years ago we moved our training exercises into town. They are going to tear down the old building to build more offices."

"Emily knows this building?"

"Yes, she trained there with the rest of us when she was a police officer. And she knows it well."

"How long until we get there?" Rick is stressed as he accelerates.

"About fifteen minutes." The sergeant alerts the rest of the team and all patrol officers in the vicinity to meet them at the warehouse.

Chapter 64
Monday 1430 Hours

Emily's mind is reeling in all different directions from the new information. She tries desperately to process everything in some logical order, but it just keeps coming back to the death of her parents. She is now staring into the eyes of her parent's killer, and it's someone that she's known for a more than a year. Someone that she has invited into her home and thought was her friend. She can't comprehend how this is possible, but the evidence of her mother's ring says differently.

Before Emily can organize her thoughts, Leo punches her in the face, and she falls backwards. From her peripheral she could see Donald take a seat to watch the performance. She was right about there being two serial killers and each one had his own demons to exercise. Her immediate aches and pains are secondary to survival. She waits for another attack from Leo because she knows his weaknesses from training, as he knows hers too.

Leo lunges forward and grabs her hair. He begins to drag her across the filthy floor. The pain is excruciating and makes thinking clearly nearly impossible. Emily takes her opportunity to grab Leo in a right wrist hold by bending his hand backwards. He instantly lets go of her as she connects a stomp kick into his groin.

Leo screams out in pain, "You bitch!"

Emily scrambles to where her gun slid into the shadows. She desperately looks for the loaded weapon, but to no avail. Leo knocks her down on her back and is on top of her wrapping his large fingers around her throat. He's preparing to strangle her out of sheer frustration and rage. Emily is no match for this muscular personal trainer. To her right, she sees one of the metal pipes. She estimates that she can't quite reach it with the tips of her fingers. The only choice she has is to dig her thumbs into Leo's face. He loosens his grip from her throat for just a moment. The room spins around her.

The oxygen begins to return to Emily's head and she begins to think more clearly. She doesn't take another moment to think, but grabs the pipe and swings it directly at Leo's head with a thud. He drops to his right side as blood gushes from his huge gapping wound. His eyes roll around in his head, and then he becomes extremely still.

Getting to her feet, Emily rushes Donald with the pipe. Her adrenaline is surging. She blinks in surprise to see Donald almost face down in a praying position and mumbling.

Emily yells, "Get up!"

As if in a trance state Donald continues to mumble an undecipherable chant, unaware of her commands.

"Get up now!" She repeats ready to strike at any moment. She wants to see his face when she bashes his skull.

Slowly Donald begins to raise his body, but instead of standing up he plunges a hunting knife into Emily's abdomen with such a force that he could barely retrieve it. Instead of finishing Emily, he decides to go to Leo. Donald drops to his murder partner's side. His demeanor changes to a concerned friend in almost a tender manner as he focuses on Leo's gushing wound. He gently tries to stop the bleeding. He feels helpless. Leo slowly begins to come around and his killer friend helps him to his feet.

Emily staggers a couple of steps as blood soaks the front of her shirt. Her body has a strange humming sensation and her legs feel weak. She knows that she doesn't stand a chance against these two men. She makes her way to the secure location of a storage closet and locks her self inside. It's the only chance she has to survive her attackers unless she bleeds to death first.

She slowly slides down the wall and sits in the corner prepared for anything that comes her way. She tries to press her right palm against the wound to slow the bleeding. It seems to help a little bit. She hears pounding noises from outside her safe haven. No doubt that the killer duo is trying to find her. She tries her cell phone again, but there is still no signal.

Emily doesn't feel scared anymore, just alone. It's a somewhat consoling feeling. Now she uses her newfound inward comfort of knowing that she isn't alone in her life anymore. Everyone has to die alone, but her comfort is knowing that she is loved. She closes her eyes and thinks about Rick and their short time together, trying desperately to relive every moment. Her body relaxes as she slumps to the side and gradually fades out of consciousness.

Chapter 65
Monday 1500 Hours

Two of the backup teams of police officers arrive just seconds before Rick and Mike screech up to the front of the building. They are then followed by several patrol officers slamming to a stop in front of the old warehouse building with sirens still blaring. Emily's rental car is parked on the far side of the building in front of a Toyota pick up truck. Rick is somewhat relived that they were correct in finding where Emily went, but terrified of what they will find inside.

All of the officers grab the appropriate shotguns from their vehicles to prepare for any type of attack; Rick and Mike follow suit. The entire law enforcement force separate, some covering the back areas, while others enter the building. Rick and Mike make their way into the main entrance.

Two patrol officers cover the back of the building just as Leo tries with slowed success to climb from a window cutting his arms and legs on the barbwire. The large muscular man continues to have some difficulty navigating himself through the opening. The officers draw down on him and get him into custody without incident. They report to the other group that one is in custody.

Mike leads the group inside the warehouse. He feels an adrenaline surge as the stakes are raised exponentially. He feels tremendously alive and glad to be a police officer at that exact moment.

Rick stays at the sergeant's side; he's not as familiar with the building and moves forward with caution. He can see why Emily would pick this old musty building to trap Donald. There are so many hiding places and ways to corner a murderous beast.

The two groups decide to split up and head in opposite directions. Before they can disperse, Donald emerges from the shadows pointing a Glock directly at the police officers and yelling some incoherent rhetoric of finally being free. Rick wasn't sure what psychopathic remark he made just before Mike unloaded two shotgun blasts at his chest. Donald was dead before he hit the ground. He was splayed out on the concrete with two large holes where his chest used to be – indeed now he was finally free.

It was over. Rick heard over the police radio that another male suspect was safely in custody. He felt relief that this whole incident was finally over and his cases were officially solved and closed forever.

Mike remains standing in the position where he fatally shot Donald. He doesn't move or even take a breath. The unsettling feelings come rushing forward that he just took another human life.

Rick gently takes the shotgun from his frozen hand. "It's okay, it was a clean shoot." He understands what the sergeant is going through. He was also involved in a shooting when he was only on the force for three years. You never get used to killing someone no matter how evil they are to society.

Two other officers quickly inspect Donald to make sure he's definitely dead. They shake their head in confirmation.

Rick realizes that he hasn't seen Emily during all of the commotion. Snapped back to reality, he says, "Where's Emily?"

The other officers begin to spread out to look for her.

Rick begins searching for her, "Emily! Emily!" He notices a hunting knife on the floor with blood on the blade. "Oh my God, Emily." He frantically searches the warehouse.

One of the patrol officers gets Rick's attention.

"Sir, there's blood over here."

Rick and the two patrol officers follow the blood trail to a closet door where it suddenly stops. He tries the doorknob, but it doesn't budge.

Rick orders, "Help me get this door open."

They begin to pry the door open with metal pieces found around the warehouse. After a little more effort the three men manage to open the door enough and then burst it wide open. Emily is slumped over in a corner with her stomach and chest soaked in crimson blood.

Rick pushes past the officers and drops to his knees. "Emily." He says gently and he cradles her in his arms. To the officers he yells, "Get an ambulance now!" He checks her pulse. It's weak, but she's alive. He tries to stop the bleeding from the deep puncture wound with pressure.

The officers call in the request immediately and then give him space.

Emily's eyes flutter open and she looks at Rick. "Hi", she says weakly. "What took you so long?"

"We got them." Rick could barely hold back his tears.

"Donald?"

"Dead."

"Good." She coughs.

"Just hold on. The ambulance is on its way."

"Rick, I want."

"It's okay just be quiet, I'm right here."

Mike appears at the doorway and sees the extent of Emily's injuries. His eyes hold Rick's grief stricken stare, and he immediately knows that it's not good news. He backs away from the door to give them privacy.

Emily begins, "No, I want you to know."

Rick interrupts, "You've got plenty of time to tell me everything. Let's just get you to the hospital first."

"Nothing in the past has mattered as much as meeting you." Her voice weakens, "You gave me life."

Rick's voice cracks, "Emily you've given me more than you'll ever know."

Emily closes her eyes and feels that everything is as it should be in her life. She squeezes Rick's hand, "I love you."

Rick hugs her close as her body goes limp in his arms.

Chapter 66
Monday 1530 Hours

High above the California rocky sea bluff soars a Peregrine Falcon. The intensely beautiful predator catches the light wind thermals as it relentlessly hunts for its next victim. It moves with the graceful speed of a well-rehearsed dancer, but with the extreme hunting skills of any large jungle cat. The falcon is one of the most feared among the bird kingdom.

Circling back around the high bluff, the falcon spots a small nesting bird with three tiny babies. It is a feast of epic proportions for the bird of prey. It gains speed and drops down on the unsuspecting mother bird. Instead of grabbing the bird by the neck in a death grip with its fierce claws, the falcon instinctively changes directions away from the nest. It continues to fly south until it's no longer visible with the naked eye. It's gone. It's finally free.

The small bird's nest with hungry babies survives without ever knowing their intended fate. Their lives continue without incident. Everything seems balanced in the bird kingdom, at least for now.

Chapter 67
Monday 1545 Hours

The law enforcement investigative spectacle moves swiftly around Mike. The ambulance and more patrol cars crowd the street around the warehouse. Mike remains numb as he leans against a patrol car, not completely aware of the events that are going on around him. Leo has been taken into custody, he stares confused at Mike through the backseat window of the patrol car. The police car slowly moves away like an old movie ending.

The coroner technicians roll a gurney out of the

warehouse with the body of Donald inside a heavy
plastic bag. The only thing that Mike can think of at
the moment is that the serial cases are finally
closed. No more women will be brutally murdered
in Santa Cruz. In his mind, he ponders, at least not
for the time being. Evil is out there in the world,
and it will eventually find its way to Santa Cruz
again, and even to a small town in Indiana. The
technicians slide the gurney into the van and shut
the doors.

Rick exits the warehouse accompanying the
gurney carrying Emily as they quickly move toward
the ambulance. Emily is extremely still and pale.
Rick is carrying several disks in his hand and spots
Mike looking completely lost and tortured. He
wished that he could change the course of the
events or turn back the clock, but the cards have already been dealt.

Rick takes a long look at Mike, only to convey
respect. Mike nods his head in recognition as Rick
disappears into the back of the ambulance. The
doors quickly shut and the emergency vehicle
speeds away with sirens blaring.

Mike stands like a statue as the crime scene continues, but his own world seems to stand still. He's
never had to draw his weapon ever in his career,
and now he's killed a man. He has to live with that
decision for the rest of his life, but the thought of
losing Emily will not be so easy. She put the lives
of others ahead of her own, and now nothing will
ever be the same again.

* * * * *

Rick watches the woman he loves narrowly hang on to life. He can barely move from his seat for fear that he would breakdown and weep. He was afraid that he wouldn't be able to stop crying once he started. He remains quiet and stares straight ahead concentrating on some inanimate object as the siren screams on toward the hospital. Rick asks himself over and over in his mind, why did this happen? It now seems crystal clear to him that he must change his entire life including his career. He will have time to think about it in upcoming weeks. The devastation he feels has left a black hole in his heart and forever in his life -- he can't lose Emily. He closes his eyes for a moment and imagines Emily walking out the warehouse safe, unhurt, and looking for him. He embraces Emily one more time in his mind.

Chapter 68
Saturday 1200 Hours

It was a beautiful sunny California day for Emily's funeral. It was fitting that it was her favorite time of year. Slowly friends left the gravesite after saying their last goodbyes. The Brandons are some of the last people to leave – it was the hardest for them to say goodbye to their dear friend and neighbor. The cemetery is now deserted.

Rick walks through the cemetery past many headstones followed closely by Sergeant. The big black Labrador takes in a few wonderful sniffs around the grassy areas and then follows Rick to Emily's grave. Her grave is located next to her Uncle Jim as requested. Rick would have thought she wanted to be buried next to her parents in Indiana, but with more thought, it was a perfect final resting place.

Rick takes a seat on the grass to think about where he's going next. He tries to think of his life as a new beginning. He has resigned from the Santa Cruz Sheriff's Office and his divorce will be final in a couple of weeks. There have been several missing person cases that have also been solved; unfortunately, they were victims of a brutal homicide. Donald had apparently been killing women for years in several different jurisdictions across California counties. It was not until the past year that he found a killing partner. Rick has some comfort in knowing that Leo won't get out of prison until the day he dies.

Rick's decision to take some time away from everything familiar to try to gain a new perspective now seems appropriate. Sergeant takes his seat next to Rick as if he too was trying to make sense of things in the world. He wills Rick to scratch his big floppy ears. Emily's neighbors accepted Rick's request to take custody of the loyal Labrador. His personal thoughts are interrupted by a familiar voice.

"Rick, it's time to go." Mike approaches Rick with a bittersweet expression on his face.

Rick stands up to greet Mike and shakes his

hand. "Nice to see you sergeant."

"Please, by now you can call me Mike."

Rick lightly laughs, "Okay, Mike."

Both men have a mutual respect for one another but desperately wish that it were under different circumstances.

"Come with me and I'll take you back to the motel." Mike heads back to his car.

Mike opens the trunk of his rental car and reveals two banker's boxes. "These are for you."

Rick replies, "I don't understand."

"Do you know what these are?"

"No."

Mike flips off one of the lids and shows many files inside. "These are Emily's files. These files are what and how Emily worked her child abduction and serial murder cases. Everything you need to know is in them."

"What can I do with them?"

"Rick, don't you understand? It's too important to have it suddenly stopped now."

"I don't know what to say."

"Just say yes." Mike shuts the trunk. "And besides, you get a perk out of the deal."

"What's that?" Rick eyes the police sergeant suspiciously.

"Me. Anytime you need any help or computer intelligence, I'm your go to guy."

"Really?"

"How else did you think that Emily was able to track down some of the most notorious child killers?" Mike never fully understood what law enforcement was all about until he met Emily. He was happy to contribute information to her ongoing cause.

Sergeant jumps into the back seat and Rick takes his seat shotgun. Mike climbs behind the wheel and sighs.

Rick turns to Mike and shakes his hand again. "Thank you, for everything."

"You just make sure that you don't lose my number." He smiles broadly as he starts the engine.

They drive in silence as the car winds around through scenic streets toward the beach. The sun brightly flashes between trees and reflects off of cars and buildings. Mike finds an available parking place in front of The Beach Motel. Rick opens the car door and steps out; he hesitates for a moment thinking about more positive memories of the motel. One of the motel room doors open and Emily steps out to greet them. She moves slowly and favors her bandaged stomach underneath her loose sweatshirt. She still looks weak but beautiful, thought Rick to himself.

Emily smiles, "So how was my funeral?"

Mike replies, "It was beautiful. You couldn't ask for a better day."

"There was a fair turnout too." Rick chimes in. He hugs Emily for a moment, not wanting to let go. She cringes in pain. "Sorry."

"It's still pretty tender." She explains.

Mike begins to transport Emily's banker boxes

into the already packed SUV. Sergeant takes his place in the back seat where there was a little bit of room left just for him.

Emily spent several days in the hospital after her life saving surgery. She had lost quite a bit of blood and sustained internal injuries, but luckily the knife wound didn't hit any major organs. It was decided by Mike and Rick that everyone would think that Emily died during surgery. It was the best way to protect Emily's identity and to keep her safe. For Emily, it was the most difficult decision she had to make because she had become very fond of her neighbors.

The couple is heading to the beautiful scenery and world-renowned wine country of Napa Valley so that Emily can fully recover from her surgery. It was a much needed rest for Rick as well. Rick's friend from the Sheriff's Office offered up the house to him for as long as he wanted. It was a perfect place to relax and figure out what would come next.

Rick takes Emily's hand, "You ready?"

"Yes."

"It will take about two and half hours to get to the house."

"It's okay." Emily replied. "We have all the time in the world."

Mike shuts the door of the SUV and walks back to the couple. "Everything's ready to go."

Emily says, "Thank you Mike so much, for everything."

"I'll take care of the house and your things. Don't worry about anything. Consider it all taken care of." He gives her a kiss on the cheek. To Rick, "You take good care of her, hear."

Rick makes a silly salute, "You got it sergeant."

Mike looked a little bit like he was going to cry, so he turns and gets back in his rental car. He hated goodbyes. Rick and Emily wave to him as he pulls away from the motel.

"You ready?" Rick asks Emily.

"More than ready." She replies.

They both get into the car and Rick pulls away from the motel and decides to take the scenic route toward the freeway to enjoy the picturesque day. The world somehow looks a little bit brighter, and perhaps a little bit more in balance than before.

Rick turns to Emily and says, "I just have one request."

"What's that?"

"You have to promise me that you'll never ever go out after a serial killer without me."

"Oh, is that all."

"Promise me."

Emily grabs his hand and states, "I promise." She looks down at her mother's ring that she now wears as a reminder of her parent's solved murder case.

Rick smiles and looks at Emily. He now knows that his life grievances are so small compared to what Emily sacrificed to help others. A child is being abducted, tortured, and murdered by a serial killer at this very moment. He knows that she won't stop hunting them as long as she has a single breath in her body. Now they will hunt down those serial killers - together.

LaVergne, TN USA
14 March 2010
175894LV00001B/14/P